D0041718

Canary
in the
Coal Mine

Madelyn Rosenberg

Holiday House / New York

CONCORDIA UNIVERSITY LIBRAR
PORTLAND, OR 97211

Text copyright © 2013 by Madelyn Rosenberg
Art copyright © 2013 by Chris Sheban
All Rights Reserved
HOLIDAY HOUSE is registered in the U.S. Patent and Trademark Office.
Printed and Bound in March 2013 at Maple Press, York, PA, USA
First Edition
1 3 5 7 9 10 8 6 4 2
www.holidayhouse.com

Library of Congress Cataloging-in-Publication Data

Rosenberg, Madelyn, 1966–
Canary in the coal mine / by Madelyn Rosenberg. — 1st ed.
p. cm.
Summary: Tired of his twelve-hour shifts and facing danger daily, Bitty, a canary whose
courage more than makes up for his small size, treks to the state capital to try to improve
working conditions in coal mines.
ISBN 978-0-8234-2600-3 (hardcover)
[1. Coal mines and mining—Fiction. 2. Canaries—Fiction. 3. Working animals—
Fiction. 4. Voyages and travels—Fiction. 5. Political activists—Fiction. 6. Animals—
Fiction. 7. West Virginia—Fiction.] I. Title.
PZ7.R71897Can 2013
[Fic]—dc23
2012033734

For Butch, Graham
and Karina—always.

Chapter 1

Bitty flattened himself against the back of the cage as the Gap-Toothed Man reached his fat hot-dog fingers through the front.

"Here, birdie, birdie," the man said. "Come on, birdie. Hurry up, now." The meaty fingers opened and closed. Bitty swerved right, then ducked low. He didn't duck low enough.

"Gotcha."

The man wrapped his fingers around Bitty's scrawny yellow neck—not choking him, but close enough—and transferred him from the wire aviary known as the Big House to a small wooden carrier. Tiny as he was, Bitty's head nearly bumped against the top. The cage swung back and forth. By the time the canary left the warm safety of Jamie's bedroom, the woozy feeling came again. Flying, what little he did of it, never bothered him, but he'd always been a lousy passenger.

"Beak up." Uncle Aubrey's voice followed them out of the bedroom, then out of the house as they lumbered toward the No. 7. "Make us proud. Remember: you're a miner."

"Yes, sir." Bitty's voice sounded more like a sick frog than anything birdlike. "As if I could ever forget," he mumbled. The Gap-Toothed Man heard him, but he didn't seem to understand any language that didn't include grunts or jokes about foreigners, which to him meant anyone without a relative working in the mines of Coalbank Hollow, West Virginia.

Uncle Aubrey couldn't hear Bitty, and that was a good thing. Bitty's uncle knew the dangers of the coal mines, but to him, that just made their work more important. With tiny marks on the larger of the aviary's two perches, he kept a tally of the lives they'd saved, the lives of men. On the other perch there was another set of tick marks for the canaries who'd lost their lives down in the No. 7. Uncle Aubrey kept that tally, too, but he didn't speak of it.

"Bitty, dear, we love you." Jamie's mother always kept the window open just a crack, and Aunt Lou's voice crept through it.

Bitty lifted a wing, not in a wave so much as a salute.

"Hope it's a gas," hollered Chester. He was the only one who ever joked about the methane and carbon monoxide that lurked in the mine's dark tunnels.

"Ouch!" Chester yelped, and Bitty knew someone had given his friend a sharp peck in the back. Bitty hoped it was Alice. Under normal circumstances, she was the nicest canary in the Big House. She was also the prettiest, and Bitty was certain he would have thought that even if she hadn't been the only female canary near his age. Bitty liked Chester, too, even with all his bad jokes. If it weren't for the two of them, he'd be stuck listening to his aunt and uncle all night, or the angry rants from Chester's mom, or the unending conversations of the rest of the dozen canaries who shared his birdseed and prison but not his point of view.

Their voices faded, replaced by the gravelly crunch of the Gap-Toothed Man's boots as they moved along the railroad tracks before the dawn.

"Mmph. You birds make some kind of racket," said the man, whose real name was Mr. Hurley. He was puffing and sputtering from the short walk. "Couldn't pay me to keep a cage that size in my bedroom. Heck, couldn't pay me to keep it in my outhouse."

A half mile later they reached the head frame, the timber structure that housed the mine's elevator, and went in. The Gap-Toothed Man found the lights and pulled the lever, sending them down the shaft.

In some mines, Bitty knew, they didn't bother taking birds in early. A lot of mines didn't bother with birds at all anymore. But the No. 7 had been gassy lately. Eight days ago, the miners had found Murray Polly laid out as if he were taking a Sunday nap with his boots on. Boggs was in a cage beside him, his toes curled, gripping an imaginary perch. The Gap-Toothed Man had other safety equipment, of course. But he always brought a bird down first.

Creeeeeeeeeeeeeeeeeeeeak. Bitty buried his head in his chest and tried to drown out the noise of the elevator as it sank into the belly of the mine. Then he shook himself, closed his eyes and sucked in a last gulp of good air. He tried to hold on to each second, stretch it like a rubber band in case it was the last second of his life. The elevator hit bottom with a clunk, and the Gap-Toothed Man pushed open the gate, holding Bitty's cage in front of him like a lantern. If the air was poison, Bitty would know it two and a half feet sooner than anybody else. His lungs were full, as if he'd swallowed a balloon.

Here goes nothing, Bitty thought. *Or everything.*

He opened his eyes and breathed in.

The breath ended in something like a hiccup. So far, the cold, damp air was safe. Bitty breathed in again, and this time the darkness didn't feel as mean. But they were just getting started. The Gap-Toothed Man held the cage at eye level so his headlamp shone in Bitty's face. "Hey, bird," he grunted. "You all right in there?"

"*Fee-yo,*" Bitty replied in a sullen monotone. *Depends on what you mean by all right,* he thought as the man held the cage out again and started a slow loop through the gloom. The light from his safety lamp bounced along the walls so that they appeared to move. The sound of dripping water echoed in the mine.

"*Fee-yo. Fee-yo. Fee-yo.*" Bitty tweeted the canary equivalent of "blah, blah, blah." Whenever he stopped tweeting, the man checked to see if he was still breathing. Then he marked the wall with a piece of chalk.

"How's the view?" The miner held the cage low to the ground, then close to the ceiling. Bitty swung back and forth again. His feathers were yellow; inside he was green.

The Gap-Toothed Man set him on the floor of the mine for a

moment and took the safety lamp from his belt. He studied the flame, then studied the bird again. He measured the airflow.

"Heigh ho, heigh ho," he finally muttered. "Reckon it's time for work."

He picked up the cage, and together they went back into the elevator. But this time they were going up.

"All right, now," the Gap-Toothed Man called to the miners who were gathering near the entrance. They rattled their lunch pails and stamped their feet to keep warm. "It's clean."

The miners surged past. A number of them carried their own canaries, but just about a dozen carried the canaries who shared the aviary owned by Jamie's family. Jamie had promised that no one else would have to lift a finger if they let him go into the canary business, but it was often Mr. Campbell who towed the birds to the mine in a little red wagon, which he covered with a burlap sack when it rained.

That was how the day began: men and birds loading into an elevator that the humans called the Cage. It was much bigger than the cage Bitty called home; still, it had earned the comparison.

"Yeoman's job, son," shouted Uncle Aubrey from a carrier that was gripped by Jamie's father. He was a tall man who had to stoop to manage the mine's low ceilings.

"Thanks."

"Bitty! Over here!"

Bitty saw Alice carried by a man the others called Rusty—for his hair, though most of the time that hair was covered with coal dust; it looked more black than red.

"All right?" she asked.

"Still kicking." Bitty did a strange tap dance that made Alice laugh, the same way she laughed when Jamie listened to Clovis Perkins, a radio comedian who made a career out of blowing his nose. A tap dance? What was he even *thinking*? "Heh-heh." He tried a laugh of his own, but that sounded strange, too, so he just waved until Alice was out of sight. Soon they were going down again, and it seemed to Bitty that his entire existence could be categorized by opposing elements: up and down. Light and dark. Alive and dead.

Chapter 2

The men set up shop in the dark bowels of the mine and began hacking away at the vein of coal that ran big and black through Audie Mountain. The Gap-Toothed Man walked among them, making notes and sniffing the air as if he, not Bitty, would be the one to detect the gas. The sounds of axes and shovels made conversation tricky. At least there was no blasting today. The canaries' job was simple: breathe and chirp. Stop, and the miners would check for bad air. That was what they called the gas that crept like a ghost through the maze of timber and tunnels. One concentrated pocket of methane and *bam*, a spark could make it blow. A pocket of odorless carbon monoxide and the miners would fall to the ground, without the *bam*, but just as dead. The canaries were supposed to be the alarm. Bad air, and they'd wobble and keel over. They'd die for real if the Gap-Toothed Man or whoever had them didn't snatch them up and get them to where the air was safe. And of course there were the times when no one could run, like the eight-days-ago accident that had killed Mr. Polly and Boggs.

Mr. Polly had been one of Jamie's most loyal customers. Boggs was just plain loyal, the sort of bird who would do you a favor and make you feel as if you'd done one for him. He was much younger than Bitty's aunt and uncle, but older than Bitty and his friends—like a big brother, the kind who teased you but taught you things, too. He was Chester's mentor when it came to jokes, the one who'd taught them that "can't cry for laughing" was better than "can't laugh for crying." Boggs could mimic Uncle Aubrey's deep voice, Aunt Lou's quaver and the bossy demands of Chester's mother. He might have had a career in radio if Doc Tatum hadn't snagged him for Jamie when he visited the general store in Wheeling. (Mr. Weymouth, who ran the company store in Coalbank Hollow, claimed to be allergic to feathers and wanted nothing to do with birds, which was why Jamie's family had been allowed to run their little side business in the first place.)

The canaries had watched the swinging cage, hypnotized, when Mr. Campbell brought Boggs home at the end of their shift. Then they'd watched Jamie slide the dead canary into one of the matchboxes he'd saved to use as a coffin. Jamie had held the funeral outside, in the darkness, and buried Boggs on the hill, where they couldn't see.

Inside the Big House, Uncle Aubrey had stood on the higher of the two perches and said a few words about service and nobility, which was the same thing he always said. He cleared his throat. "May his spirit soar."

"May his spirit soar," the canaries repeated. Uncle Aubrey had scratched another mark onto the perch, and they'd retreated into silence. Bitty wished for that silence now, instead of the scraping and clanging of the mine.

His shift would likely last eleven hours, but already it felt as if they'd been down there for ten.

"You've got to find your happy place, that's all," Aunt Lou said whenever Bitty complained. He supposed she meant the aviary, but that wasn't exactly full of wonderful memories. He had friends there, and his aunt and uncle, of course. But there was a constant reminder of those who were *not* there. His father, who had died in the mines with Chester's father, had been buried before Bitty even hatched out. His mother had lived to see Bitty and name him, before she died a week later of a broken heart. (Uncle Aubrey said it was technically dehydration because the broken heart kept her from eating and drinking, but that didn't change the outcome.) Dickens and Fern had been gone two seasons already. And now they'd lost Boggs, whose death (or Mr. Polly's, anyway) barely got a mention in the city paper. It was the big disasters—like the one in Everettville that killed ninety-seven men, or the one in Jed that killed eighty—that took the headlines and lived on in the songs Mrs. Campbell sang in a minor key.

The Gap-Toothed Man stared into the cage, and Bitty gave him an obligatory chirp, inhaling a mouthful of coal dust. He chirped again. With each *fee-yo*, he tried to remember something about his mother.

"*Fee-yo.*" She smelled like sunflower seeds.

"*Fee-yo.*" She was yellow, like Bitty, only her wings were brown, sort of a sunflower in reverse.

"*Fee-yo.*" He wondered if she ever sang, like Mrs. Campbell. Bitty didn't think so.

Canaries were known for making music, but the canaries in the No. 7 rarely went beyond their steady *fee-yo*, like a telegraph repeating the same message in Morse code. They never even sang when they were happy, not that they were happy often, with the exception of Aunt Lou. No, Bitty didn't have a happy place. He had a cold, dark, angry place, and he wanted to get out before they carried him out like Boggs in a matchbox coffin.

The question was how to escape. The aviary was locked from the outside with a long metal bar. Bitty couldn't move it. He'd tried. The door opened in the early morning, when it was time for work. It opened at night when Mr. Campbell brought them home again. But the Campbells had quick hands. The door snapped shut in the time it would take to whack a fly.

Bitty tried to think of another way out, but the mine wasn't con-ducive to heavy thinking. Thoughts passed through his brain slowly, as if he had to dig for them. Time passed slowly, too. If there'd been a clock, the hands would have moved backward.

The men stopped to eat and drink. The Gap-Toothed Man made another loop through the mine to test the air quality, but not before dropping a chunk of onion sandwich into Bitty's cage. Whoever worked with Rusty got the best meals, but lately even those meals had been lacking. There were still biscuits, but without honey. Fruit this month had consisted of stewed prunes.

Inhale.

Tick.

Exhale.

Tock.

At last the whistle blew. Up they went, and then out into the mountain air. The men left the cages with Mr. Campbell, who stacked them on the wagon.

"Thanks," Mr. Campbell said as the Gap-Toothed Man handed him the cage with Bitty inside.

"Hope your boy's giving you a cut," the miner replied.

Bitty looked around as the cages were stacked beside him and up above. It was hard to see whether everyone was there, but he could see Mr. Campbell's lips moving as he counted the birds. Aunt Lou took roll, like a schoolteacher.

"Aubrey?"

"Here."

"Crockett?"

"Here."

"Hazel?"

"Here."

"Chester?"

"Ho!"

Bitty could just make out Chester's left foot in the cage diagonally above him. Then the foot disappeared, replaced by Chester's upside-down head.

"Sleeping on the job again?" Bitty asked him.

"Very funny. Speaking of which: Where does a five-hundred-pound canary sit?"

"Where?" Bitty asked, though he'd heard this one. It had been one of Boggs's favorites.

"Anywhere he wants to." Chester delivered the punch line so solemnly that to Bitty it sounded less like a joke and more like a call to action.

Chapter 3

Mr. Campbell pulled the birds back along the railroad tracks and into the light of Jamie's tiny bedroom, which was clean, unless you looked under the bed.

"Everybody here?" Jamie asked his pa.

"Every one." Mr. Campbell's smile was as worn as his overalls.

"Good," Jamie said.

Good, Bitty thought.

One by one, Jamie unlocked the small carriers and slid each bird back into the Big House, which rested on a board-and-cinder-block table so that it was even with the bed. "There you go. That's a boy."

After the small carrier, the aviary felt big, and it looked big, too, though that was mostly because of the smallness of Jamie's bedroom; the Big House was the only piece of furniture in there besides the bed and a small, wobbly nightstand.

"Make sure to wash those hands before dinner," Mrs. Campbell called from the kitchen. Jamie followed her voice out of the room to find a washbasin.

"Thought he'd never leave," Chester said. As much as the canaries liked Jamie, they were glad of time alone. While they'd been out, Jamie's mother had changed the newspaper that lined their cage. Bitty kicked some hay and sawdust out of the way to check the date in the corner: Sunday, March 1, 1931. It was a few days old, according to the calendar in Bitty's head, but Mrs. Campbell had given them the Charleston paper instead of the thin *Coalbank Chronicle*. And she'd saved them the news section! You couldn't always count on Mrs. Campbell to line the cage with the sections that mattered. Some days, she gave them Fashion. What did Bitty care about permanent waves or the proper length of a lady's skirt? Come to think of it, what did Mrs. Campbell care? She didn't have money for those things. And don't even get him started on all the advertisements for tonics and tablets guaranteed to ward off biliousness and promote regularity. *Humans.*

"Anything good?" Chester asked.

Bitty scanned the page. "How about this? 'Dog Saves Owner from Fire.' A Dalmatian. They're giving him a medal for valor."

"Medal," scoffed Uncle Aubrey. "What'd he save, one man?"

"Yeah, but he was blind," Bitty said, reading the next two paragraphs. "The man, not the dog."

"*One* man," said Uncle Aubrey. "We save more than that every day. But do we get a medal? No, sir."

"Now, dear," broke in Aunt Lou. "What would we even *do* with a medal?"

"I don't suppose there's anything about…about Boggs?" Alice asked. "Or Mr. Polly?"

"That'd be old news by now," Bitty said.

"Where's the flying forecast?" asked Chester, changing the subject.

Bitty, a faster reader, found it first, partly obscured by the water dish. He and Chester always read the flying forecast, even though it was for planes and crop dusters, and even though they never actually flew anywhere.

"Clear skies," Bitty said. "Winds from the northeast diminishing at a thousand feet."

They were quiet, imagining what it would feel like to fly that high. They had never been one hundred feet in the air. Or even ten.

In the next room, Jamie's father asked for the beans. The canaries heard him clearly through the thin walls. "Pass the corn bread, too, while you're at it."

"Beans again?" said Jamie. Bitty could picture them sitting in those straight-backed chairs around the small table he'd seen on his trips in and out of the house. The room also held the Crosley radio that had been a gift from Mrs. Campbell's parents. It was cheap as far as radios went, boxy instead of cathedral style. Still, the Campbells had almost sold it three times.

"You'll eat those beans and smile," Clayton Campbell said.

"Yes, sir."

"Now, me," continued Mr. Campbell, his voice suddenly lighter, "I like beans. That's why I married you, Mary. The day I saw you I said, 'Now, there's a woman who knows how to dress up a bean.' Pass the Tabasco."

"Look," said Jamie. "This bean's wearing a suit. Get it? He's dressed up!"

"Try using your fork along with your imagination," his mother said. "There's pickled corn, too, Jamie."

"You want time to use your imagination, you should come work with me," Mr. Campbell said. "Plenty of time for thinking."

"But Pa—" Jamie didn't have a chance to say anything else.

"Other boys are leaving school," Mr. Campbell said. "Trying to, anyway. Jason Carter's a trapper and he's just a little older than you are."

Mrs. Campbell's voice frosted over. "You want him to end up without a right arm, like the Wasserman boy? You want him trapped down there, writing his last words with a nub of coal? 'See you in heaven, Pa?' He's finishing school. Clay, we talked about this. I'll eat beans forever if that's what it takes."

"I go down there every day, Mary. I've still got both my arms." Bitty imagined Mr. Campbell flapping them, like wings.

"Tell me it's safe, Clayton."

"It's good work with good men," Jamie's father said, sounding like Uncle Aubrey. "It's proud work. I like it better than any job I've ever had."

"Tell me it's safe."

There was silence after that, interrupted by the clatter of silverware.

"Well," Mr. Campbell said finally. "It's not like demand's up. There's thousands of miners wanting for jobs, and grown men at that."

They started talking again, but there was no more laughter. Bitty wished for a closed door and thicker walls. Jamie had pasted comics all over his room for both decoration and insulation, but they didn't do a thing to block out the sound. At night, Mr. Campbell's snoring filled every cranny of the three-room house.

Bitty shook himself and got in line for the chipped china water bowl. When it was his turn, he leaned back his head and gargled, hoping for the sweet taste of a mountain spring. The only flavor he could identify was coal.

"What a day," Uncle Aubrey said from his perch.

"Same as every other day," Bitty mumbled.

Chester shook his head. "Why don't you just sleep when we're down there? It makes the time go faster."

"Oh, gee, I don't know. Because when you sleep, they think you're dead?" Bitty said.

"Oh, so that's why they're always poking me. Sleep with your eyes open."

"Sleep. Work," Bitty said. "The Big House is the right name for this place. Just call me One Forty-Six from now on."

"What's One Forty-Six?"

"My prison number. In human prisons they call you by a number instead of a name. It was in the *Gazette*."

"Jamie doesn't call you One Forty-Six, does he?" Chester said. "So it's not a prison, is it?"

Jamie had his own special name for Bitty: Big Yellow. The "big" part was a joke, of course. Bitty was shorter, by half an inch, than any other bird in the aviary, including Alice. It might as well have been a foot. But joke or not, it wasn't a number.

"See?" Chester said. "You know I'm right."

"Well, it feels like a prison," Bitty said. He drew himself up to his full height. "I'm thinking about busting out."

Chapter 4

"Sure you are," Chester said.

"Well, I am," Bitty said.

"You wouldn't leave."

"I would."

"But don't you remember..." Chester paused and looked around. Then he whispered another name they all knew: "Hubert?"

Hubert was the only bird who had ever escaped the Big House. He'd done it the previous spring, by way of a loose screw on a door hinge. The rest of them had watched as he flew out Jamie's window and into the warmth of a Sunday. There'd been one glorious moment when he'd looked back at them, his face alight with freedom and sunshine. The next moment a dark shadow had swooped over him. A Cooper's hawk. There was a flash of color as the hawk grabbed Hubert in her talons and squeezed.

They never saw Hubert again. They never saw the hawk again, either, but they knew she was out there. Cipher. That was the hawk's name. Jamie had taken her in not long before Hubert's demise. She slept in a cage near the canaries for a week while Jamie mended her fractured wing. She'd spoken only once during that time, to say her name. The rest of the time she'd been still, as if she'd been carved from granite.

"You should really consider becoming a vegetarian," Hubert had called to her one day.

"This is grade-A canary you're looking at, toots," he called the next. He nodded at Bitty and Chester. "They're grade B."

He'd called her names. Bird Breath and Talon Toes were his favorites, along with Predator, which he uttered like a curse.

Jamie had walked into the room just as the hawk lunged, denting the bars of her cage.

"Whoa, now, hang on." Jamie turned to the canaries. "Sorry. It's not fair to make you spend all day in the mines and all night next to her." He turned to the hawk, who had gone back to her granite-like pose, though her red eyes missed nothing. "I thought you were going to be *good*." The red eyes bored into the canaries. Even with the bars and Jamie between, it didn't seem like enough.

"I wish my ma would let you stay in the front room," Jamie told the hawk. "I'll have to take you outside." And he'd carried her into the cold evening.

The hawk was restless on the porch. Jamie had been forced to release her before she'd completely healed. Her wing tipped up at the end in a kind of wave, which was how the canaries recognized her the day Hubert—to quote Aunt Lou—"went to his reward."

Dinner was over.

Jamie came in, flopped on his bed and stared at the ceiling. Then he rolled over and looked at his birds. Bitty pressed his beak against the bars, which had once been a brassy gold but were now tarnished and nearly brown.

"I know just how you feel in there, Big Yellow," Jamie said.

Hardly, Bitty thought. Jamie was allowed to walk around in the world, wasn't he? Jamie got to see sunlight. The boy reached out with his index finger and touched the canary's head, just above the eyes.

"Nah," Chester whispered. "You'd never leave. Anyway, it'll be spring soon. It's nice here in the spring."

But that was where Chester was wrong.

"It isn't nice here in the spring," Bitty said. "It isn't *anything* here in the spring. Spring's out there, where the world is."

Together they looked through the window at the strong,

unmoving backside of the mountain. Two turkey buzzards sailed like paper airplanes along the darkened ridge.

"Spring is where *they* are," Bitty said.

"Yeah, but look at them. They can take care of themselves. You're little. Bite-size. You'd be hawk food in no time."

Bitty supposed he should be used to it. His mother had called him "a bitty thing" from the moment he hatched—the only egg to open out of a clutch of four.

"He may be small, but he dreams big." Alice joined in the whispered conversation. She looked like springtime herself, with feathers the color of mustard flowers.

"Thanks," Bitty said. "I think."

"But Ches has a point. Wouldn't you be scared out there? Remember the hawk—"

"I'm scared *in here*," Bitty interrupted. "Especially after what happened to Boggs." He wished Alice would come up with a nickname for him the way she had for Chester, though it was probably just as well that she didn't call him Bit.

"We don't even know what happened to Boggs," Alice said. "It could have been lots of things."

"Exactly," Bitty said. It made him think of "Gone, Birdie, Gone," a nursery rhyme they'd learned when they were younger:

If the dust don't get you
If the beam don't fall
If the gas don't take you
'Fore the whistle's call
If your breath don't rattle
If your bones don't shake
Then you're gone, birdie, gone
Never more to WAKE!

The canaries always yelled out the "wake" part as loudly as they could. Then they fell to the ground, the way human children fell when they played Ring Around the Rosie, though they forgot (like the human children) that the falling down part actually meant death. Bitty couldn't forget it now. He was haunted by the poem's words, by the truth of them.

"You know, it wouldn't be so scary if we were all out there together," he said. He tried to make it sound offhand, as if he hadn't imagined the three of them soaring out the window in a tiny, perfect V. "You guys could come with me. We'd have an adventure. Bona fide."

If there was one thing the birds in the Big House knew about, it was adventure. In the stories Jamie read out loud to them, humans were always sneaking aboard pirate ships or fighting with magic swords.

"What would we eat?" Alice asked, sweeping her wing through some round seeds that had dropped from the feeder. Charleston's Finest, that was the brand.

"Eat?"

"Just say, for the sake of argument, that we did go with you. What would we eat?"

"We'd eat corn—not that pickled stuff, we'd eat it fresh off the stalk. Or worms." Alice made a face. "Okay, not worms, then," Bitty said. "Wildflowers." He tried on the French accent he'd overheard on one of Mrs. Campbell's radio shows. "Would you care for a plate of violets, Mademoiselle?"

"*Merci.*"

"I'll bet everything tastes better when you're free," Bitty said.

"Where would we sleep?" asked Chester.

"Trees," Bitty said. "We'll build nests. Really comfortable nests, with cotton and straw and leaves."

"Like you know all about it. What about work?" Chester had spent most of his life trying to get out of work; still, it was a valid question.

"We'll find new work," Bitty said, scooting over so that his feet partially covered up the words *unemployment soars* in a *Gazette* headline. "Come on, Chester, haven't you ever wanted to be something besides a miner?"

"I wanted to be a singer," Alice broke in. "You probably think that's stupid."

"It's not stupid." Among the canaries who did bother to sing, it was the males who always did it best, but no matter. Bitty looked Alice in the eye to show her how not-stupid he thought she was. Now he understood why she always threw in a few trills with her *fee-yos.* "How about it, Chester? There's got to be something else you want to do."

"I'd like to be a taste-tester for a birdseed company," he said.

They laughed, but they stopped when Jamie looked at them funny. The boy needed a haircut, and it wouldn't be long before Mrs. Campbell put one of her mixing bowls on his head and cut around it.

"You weren't talking about me, were you?" Jamie asked, counting the birds again. Without Boggs, they were an unlucky thirteen, though Bitty knew Jamie had already talked to Doc Tatum about finding a replacement.

The boy sprinkled some extra seed through the wire. Then he pulled out a book and began to read aloud. "*The Adventures of Tom Sawyer.* Chapter eight."

"You wouldn't leave," Chester whispered, moving closer to Bitty. "Anyway, you should never bite the hand that feeds you."

"No," Bitty repeated. "You should never..."

But then he stopped. He had a plan.

Chapter 5

It was the wind that told Bitty when to go, but a newspaper article told him where.

The article was in the *Coalbank Chronicle*, which was full of the most boring news possible: "Flora Hoffsetter Visits Niece" and "Kiwanis Club Meets Tuesday." But when he saw "Little Sammy Visits Legislature," he read beyond the headline.

> Little Sammy Sowers, age 4, visited the still-under-construction Capitol this week with his proud parents. The family also stopped at the Court-house, where the legislature is meeting while workers put finishing touches on the Capitol complex, the original building having been destroyed by fire. Imagine their surprise when Del. Abbot Allman invited the rosy-cheeked tyke to the floor and asked him what he wanted the legislature to do for him this term.
>
> "I want chocolate," Sammy said.
>
> Del. Allman made the boy an honorary page and gave him a chocolate bar before the family departed for the home of their cousins, the Willard F Scruggs Family of McCormick Street.

Okay, so maybe it wasn't a huge thing, a four-year-old kid asking the state government for a bar of chocolate. *But he got it.* If a four-year-old could go to Charleston, ask for something and get it, maybe Bitty could ask for something, too. He knew that legislators spoke their own language—"political jibber jabber" Mr. Campbell called it. And their Bird probably wasn't any better than the Gap-Toothed Man's. But there were other ways of communicating, like the way Mrs. Campbell's eyes told Jamie he'd pushed things too far, or the way Mr. Campbell's boots, when he took them off on the front porch, foretold anything from payday (a gentle thud, followed by a light step into the house) to an accident (heavy thud, slow-moving feet). If Bitty could just make it to Charleston, he could visit those legislators and find a way to get through to them. He could convince them to make things safer for the Coalbank Hollow canaries—and for the men in the No. 7. Well, *maybe* he could.

"Who do you think you are? Mother Jones?" Chester asked. "Hey—I saw an advertisement for a long black dress, if you're looking."

"I'm not looking," Bitty said. The late Mrs. Jones had tried to help the Coalbank miners fight for better conditions and pay. She'd tried to do the same across the state, and Bitty's father had even broken his no-singing policy to learn some of her union songs. But the company had threatened to fire anyone who joined up—and then had made good on the threat. After that, a war of words had turned into a real war between miners and coal operators, along with their hired guns from the Baldwin-Felts Detective Agency. In the years since, the Coalbank miners had let the idea of a union die, like the embers in Mrs. Campbell's potbellied stove. Every few months, the idea would spark up again, then grow cold.

Oh, come on. Who was he fooling? If Mother Jones couldn't do it, how could he? She'd been a leader. Bitty couldn't even lead his two best friends out of a cage.

On the other hand, the mine wars were old news. The miners' problems—and the canaries' problems—were still current events. Bitty thought about the reports the Gap-Toothed Man had filed.

Requests for support beams that were sent back with notes that said "Buy 'em yourself" (which he did). Notices about a broken booster fan that was never fixed. Coal dust that he watered like lettuce seed. Bitty thought about his parents. And Boggs. Maybe it was time for someone to try again.

"That kid was only four years old and he got people to listen," Bitty said.

"That kid was human," Chester said. "And Mother Jones didn't exactly have feathers, either."

"Well I can try," Bitty said. "That's something."

"It ain't much."

"Oh, quiet, Ches," said Alice. "It's a start, isn't it? You should go, Bitty. You could change things."

"Sure," Chester said. "Go. Write a bill. Protest. Like nobody's tried that before."

"Well, why couldn't he?" piped up Aunt Lou, who was within earshot. "Not that he's going anywhere, mind, but if he did..."

"He's a miner." Old Bird Crockett rarely spoke, and his voice came out in a wheeze. "Miners have as much pull with the government as an ant has with an anteater."

"I just want to get a message to Charleston," Bitty said. "And let them know how bad it all is."

"Don't you think they already know?" Crockett asked.

"Then I'll tell them again."

Waiting was the hard part.

To put his plan into action, Bitty needed an open window, and that meant he needed to wait until Mrs. Campbell thought it was warm enough to raise the windows more than her usual half an inch "for health reasons." Springtime came later to the mountains than it did to the rest of the country, but already, Bitty could see signs of it. The robins were back. The Campbells' yard was full of green sprouts where Jamie's mother had planted crocuses everywhere that wasn't already being used to grow carrots, beets, peas or potatoes.

When the flowers opened, the nights would be gentler. Then Bitty would go. At first it seemed as if March would never shift from lion to lamb. But before Bitty crossed the last day off the calendar in his head, the weather changed. The crocuses bloomed yellow and purple. Jamie oiled his baseball glove, and Mrs. Campbell hummed more often.

"Cleaning day," she announced one morning. Usually she waited until the birds were gone to begin her chores, but this day, she snatched the rag rug next to Jamie's bed so she could take it outside to shake it. Like the rug in the main room, it was braided with strips of colored fabric, which made it harder to notice the coal dust.

"Gee, it's too bad I have school," Jamie coughed under the covers.

"Plenty for you to do when you get home," Mrs. Campbell said cheerfully. Jamie got up and she yanked the sheets off his bed.

That night, Bitty felt the wind, more of it than usual, pouring through the gap beneath the window. The sash was a full three inches high: the perfect height.

"This is it," Bitty announced. "My last night in a cage."

"Oh, dear. What would your mother say?" Aunt Lou asked.

Bitty rolled his inky-black eyes. "I told you, Aunt Lou: I've got to make it to Charleston before something else goes wrong." That was the way Aunt Lou always put it herself: his father had gone into the mine and *something went wrong*. Four canaries were supposed to hatch *but something went wrong*. Well, Bitty was going to go pay a visit to those legislators before something went wrong with him. He'd let them know—he'd let everyone know—how unfair it all was. If he could help the miners, they would help the canaries. It was his mission and he was assigning it to himself, even if it wasn't officially endorsed by Uncle Aubrey.

"This is crazy talk," Uncle Aubrey said. "*Think*, son. You don't up and quit a job in the middle of a depression! Once a miner bird, always a miner bird."

Aunt Lou's arguments weren't as loud, but they were still fiery. "We could organize! 'Birds of a feather, fight together!'"

But a union wasn't for birds; it was for free men in better times. People had died trying to build up the union in West Virginia. Those miners who hadn't surrendered at Blair Mountain? It wasn't gas that killed them; it was guns. No canary could have saved them. And tensions still ran high.

Uncle Aubrey made one final speech. "Canaries aren't quitters," he said. "Three times I've been knocked out in that mine, but I didn't quit."

"I'm not saying it's not good work," Bitty said (though he was thinking it).

"No respect for history," Uncle Aubrey said. "Miner bird. Now, there's a title that means something."

"I respect history; I just don't want to *be* history. I'm going to make things better. You'll see." As Bitty said it, he couldn't help thinking of everyone—the union men, his own father—who had tried to make things better but had ended up the worse for it.

"Do you think you'll be warm enough?" Aunt Lou asked. She dropped her voice to a whisper. "And Bitty, do be careful of that hawk. She's crazy as a bedbug. There's something about her that's not quite right."

"Don't worry," Bitty said. He outlined his plan again. Aunt Lou listened. So did the other birds, though they kept their distance, as if he had canary pox. Uncle Aubrey pretended to be stone deaf, but the feathers around his neck stuck out like spikes.

"I could hold off a day, if someone wanted to come along," Bitty finished. He looked up at the perch where Alice and Chester were swinging.

"That's enough, mister," Alice's mother snapped. "*That* someone isn't going anywhere!"

"Likewise," said Chester's mother. "My boy knows where he belongs. He's not above his raising."

"I didn't mean...," Bitty said. But it was no use. You didn't have to have a mother to know you couldn't argue with one. He walked to a quiet corner of the cage and turned his back until he heard the flutter of wings.

"You're pretty brave," Alice said.

"I'm pretty scared, if you want to know the truth."

"Bitty, I wish..." But she didn't finish, and he looked away.

It was better not to talk. He took Chester's advice and pretended to sleep. Finally, he heard Alice flit back to her mother. He opened his eyes again to look at Jamie, asleep for real in his narrow bed. The boy was thirteen times taller than he was, but because he was sleeping, Bitty felt protective. "I'll miss you," he said. "All of you." His beak didn't move when he spoke. His voice was so soft, it could have been a breeze.

Chapter 6

At last, it was morning. The heavy rap on the door of Jamie's bedroom started Bitty's heart pounding.

"Come in!" Jamie covered up a yawn as the Gap-Toothed Man approached the cage.

"Think I smelled some of your ma's oatmeal out in the kitchen," the miner said. "Now, if that don't get you moving, I don't know what will."

"Eggs," said Jamie. The canaries shuddered, just hearing the word, as the boy continued: "Bacon. Toast. Sausage. Apple pie."

"Okay, now, who's ready for work?" the Gap-Toothed Man asked. He sprinkled some birdseed at the back of the cage. It was the trick he always used to get them away from the door, but it was good seed so most of the time the canaries played along. The fingers came through the door next, and there was the usual fluttering as the birds tried to avoid them. But this time, Bitty didn't duck. He darted into the miner's open hand.

"Eager one this morning," the Gap-Toothed Man said. "Hey, Jamie. You hear about the miner from Beckley?"

"Is this a joke, Mr. Hurley, or a true story?"

If Bitty was lucky, he could escape before he was ever stuffed into the carrying cage—maybe even before Mr. Hurley delivered his punchline. The canary opened his mouth wide, but the miner tightened his grip. Bitty couldn't move. He'd have to switch to plan B.

"So this miner from Beckley falls down a shaft," the Gap-Toothed Man continued. "And his boss yells down after him: 'You break anything?' And the miner says 'Nope. Ain't nothing down here to break.'"

The Gap-Toothed Man laughed and stuffed Bitty into the carrier. When he withdrew his hand, Bitty breathed in huge gulps of air.

"Bet they tell it different in Beckley," Jamie said.

"Bet they do, at that," the Gap-Toothed Man said. He turned and clomped off in his heavy boots, the carrier dangling from his hand like an apple on a tree. The Big House was quiet another moment. Then it sprang to life.

"Beak up, son," Uncle Aubrey called through the open window.

"We love you, Bitty," Aunt Lou said. "Enjoy the world!"

And then, from Alice: "Be brave."

"Good-bye," Bitty called, hoping the wind would carry his voice back to the house. "Good-bye!"

For the first time on the walk to the No. 7 mine, Bitty wasn't afraid. Down went the elevator. Up went his stomach, somewhere into his throat. Bitty listened to the sound of Mr. Hurley's breathing, and to the dripping noises deep in the mine. He held his own breath, felt the swelling of his chest. And then? He breathed, regular and safe, in the darkness.

Now it was time for action.

As the Gap-Toothed Man started his loop, Bitty dropped to the floor of the cage, closed his eyes and pointed his feet—which were small, like the rest of him—straight up in the air.

He held his breath again as the Gap-Toothed Man lifted the bamboo cage so he could study the condition of the canary inside.

"Vents!" the Gap-Toothed Man hollered, even though he was the only one in the mine. He thundered toward the elevator and pulled the switch. "Vents!" The elevator went up. The Gap-Toothed Man pushed open the gate, and Bitty felt the fresh, clean air of the outside. "Somebody turn on those fans!" The workers who had been standing outside grumbled—if they didn't work they didn't get paid, and there would be no work for a couple of hours, at least. A canary was dead. There was gas in the mine.

The Gap-Toothed Man walked over to Clayton Campbell, who was already packing the rest of the canaries into his red wagon.

"Can't leave them out in the cold all morning," Mr. Campbell explained. "They'll catch their death. You let me know when it's clear."

"Will do," said the Gap-Toothed Man. "Leave me one of them live birds, would you? You can have this one." He handed Mr. Campbell the cage with Bitty inside. Wait, this wasn't the way it was supposed to work. The Gap-Toothed Man was supposed to open the cage and take Bitty out so that Bitty could nick him on the hand and soar into the springtime. Plan C, then? Bitty kept his eyes closed. He felt himself swing in Mr. Campbell's hand. He heard Alice say "Is he really...?"

"Easy," Chester said. "He's faking it. I think."

Bitty wanted to answer, but he didn't dare. He listened to Mr. Campbell's footsteps, the bump of the wagon and the opening and closing of a door. He felt the warmth of the Campbells' house.

"Clay?" Mrs. Campbell said. "What's wrong?"

"Bad air," Mr. Campbell told her. "Jamie left for school yet?"

"He's still in his room."

Bitty felt himself carried a few more feet, and then he heard Mr. Campbell's funeral knock on Jamie's bedroom door.

"Come in," Jamie called.

Mr. Campbell held out the carrier with Bitty inside. "Sorry, son."

"It's Big Yellow," Jamie said, a hitch in his voice.

"Special, was he?"

"He was...my favorite."

"You're not supposed to get attached," Mr. Campbell said. "But I guess that's like telling a dog not to eat."

In the carrier, Bitty worked hard to keep still. The cage door opened and he felt Jamie's hand, so much gentler than the Gap-Toothed Man's, pull him out. The hand held him loosely and carefully. Bitty opened his left eye. Jamie's other hand held a matchbox coffin.

"Easy now," Jamie said.

Bitty opened his right eye. This wasn't the way he'd planned it, but he had no choice. *Sorry, Jamie,* he said inside his head. *I'm really, really sorry.* Then he opened his beak and chomped down hard on the pocket of flesh between the thumb and first finger of Jamie's right hand.

Chapter 7

"Hey!" Jamie said, jerking his hand back. "For crying out...*Ouch!*"

He dropped Bitty and sent him tumbling toward the ground. Quickly, the canary flapped his wings and righted himself, then zoomed forward in flight, away from Jamie's hand, away from the coffin. It was a small room, and Bitty couldn't have been more than five feet from the open window. Still, it was the farthest stretch he had ever flown. The window loomed in front of him like an open mouth. Everything looked bigger, now that the bars of the cage weren't breaking his view into small chunks.

The other birds cheered as Bitty got closer to the window. He recognized Chester's war whoop and a "Mercy!" from Aunt Lou. He wondered if she was twitching her tail feathers the way she always did when she got excited, but he didn't have time to check. "Right foolishness, that's what this is; his father was like that," Uncle Aubrey said to nobody in particular.

"What in the world?" Jamie's mother heard the noise from the kitchen. By the time she got to Jamie's bedroom, Bitty was slipping through the open window and out of the house.

Once he reached the cool, bracing air, Bitty scanned the sky and trees for signs of the Cooper's hawk. All was clear. Only then did he dare to look back. He saw his family and friends watching through a grid of bars and glass. Jamie was watching, too, smiling a little as he shook his sore hand. The way he was shaking it, he appeared to be waving good-bye. Bitty wanted to wave back. He wanted to apologize, out loud instead of in his head. But he didn't stop.

Free!

Bitty stretched his wings as far as they could go, and for once, he touched not Chester, not some dangling perch or metal bar, but pure spring air. He tried out one of Chester's war whoops. *"Whooooo-eeee!"* Then he threw in some extra whoops of his own. Pumping his wings as quickly as he could, he circled the house and tried to find a rhythm for his flight. The wind slid over his feathers, and under them. He looked down.

The Campbells lived in a company house, which meant it had been built—quickly and cheaply—by the mining company. Rent came straight from Mr. Campbell's paycheck, when there was one. The cost was reasonable enough, but the house didn't come with "modern conveniences," and the lease had a list of rules a mile long. There was just enough room for Jamie's family—though last summer, during the drought, the Campbells had "let out" Jamie's room to two bachelor miners, and Jamie and the birds had taken over a corner in the main room near the radio.

The Campbells' house was nearly identical to all of the other houses that were lined up like ducks on the narrow strip of land between the train tracks and the mountain. It was small and box-like, with a sharp roof so the snow would slide off. Like the neighbors' houses, it was more gray than white. But when Bitty looked carefully, he found things that made Jamie's house different. All those crocuses in the yard, for one thing, and a dogwood tree in the back, with a trunk that twisted and turned as if it couldn't decide which way to grow. Bitty took note of everything: of the twisted tree, of the door Jamie's mother had painted blue, a strike against dull, gray February. (She'd promised the coal company that she'd paint it white again when the Campbells moved on.)

Bitty repeated the address to himself four times: 212 Slusser Road, Coalbank Hollow, West Virginia. He wasn't sure which way he needed to go to get to Charleston, but Uncle Aubrey had told him once: "If you don't know where you're going, at least make sure you know where you've been." Now he knew.

He angled himself downward and snatched a purple crocus from the yard, holding it tight in his beak. Before he went anywhere, he had a stop to make: the hill where Jamie buried the birds who didn't survive. Bitty had heard Jamie speak of the burial hill, but he had never seen it. That must be it, next to the creek. Small sticks, rising from the ground like fingers, marked each grave as if to say "Here I am." One of those sticks must mark his mother's grave, and one his father's, but it was impossible to tell which. And there was one stick greener than the rest. Boggs. Bitty flew over the markers and let the crocus drop. It landed nearly upright. From the sky, it looked as if it were growing there.

"Every one of those birds did important work," Uncle Aubrey always said. Bitty had some important work to do, too. It was time to start.

He followed the train tracks and headed north, pausing when he reached the mine's dark entrance. That was the part he recognized. But he'd never seen the tipple, used to load coal into rail cars, standing tall against the greening mountain. It looked like a roller coaster from one of Jamie's picture postcards.

All was quiet at the tipple and at the mine. The men were drinking their coffee, activity suspended for the morning because they thought Bitty was dead. He flew on before they noticed him, abandoning the tracks for Coalbank Hollow's Main Street. There was the company store, where his birdseed, Mr. Campbell's boots, the mail, the beans and almost everything else in the house came from, all costing dearly, as if the people who shopped there were Rockefellers instead of coal miners. Mr. Campbell was paid in scrip, special coins that were issued by the mine instead of cash; this was the only place he could spend his earnings. Bitty had seen some scrip in Jamie's room. It had the name of the coal company stamped on the front, with a hole punched in the middle, as if someone had punched the value right out of it.

Still, Mr. Weymouth, who ran the store, looked like a grandfather, not the sort of person who tried to pinch people, which was how Mrs. Campbell described him. The window was freshly cleaned, and Bitty hovered for a moment, staring through it. Everything in the coal camp seemed new, and that kept Bitty's wings pumping strongly for a while. Flying—really *flying*—was everything he and Chester had imagined it would be. But when the farthest you're used to going is a few feet in a cage, one mile can feel like ten. Bitty's wings hurt. The air stung his throat. He found a tree and rested, watching the limbs above him for hawks. For a moment, he dared to close his eyes, enjoying the feel of the smooth bark beneath his feet. But with his eyes closed, he saw the faces of his friends.

He blinked them away. "I'm not going to be homesick for a cage," he told himself. "Not yet." He started flying again and made it as far as the next large oak. He should have done some training. All those boring hours in the mine? He could have been flapping his wings, building up muscle. Now it was too late.

He looked around at the endless trees, the waves of mountains and the steady stitches of train track. The train! Maybe he could find a seat on a coal car! Then he could ride to the city in style. Because it wasn't just his aching wings he was worried about. The sun, though it was shining now, would disappear like a lemon drop. The night would be cold, and the hawk would be stalking her dinner. And then there was his own food to think about. He'd talked a good game about corn and wildflowers, but he didn't know where to find either one, especially not in late March. He hadn't even made a flight plan. Until now, freedom itself had seemed like his destination.

Taking the train sounded like a proper strategy, at least, so he returned to the tracks and followed them to the freight station near the mine. The only trains there now were on sidetracks, broken down and headed nowhere.

Bitty stamped his foot. Now that he'd found the station, he didn't want to wait; he wanted to *move*. He paced up and down along the gutter above the depot. What if the train didn't come for hours? What if it didn't come for *days*? He'd often heard the whistle and seen the train as it rumbled by Jamie's bedroom. But he hadn't ever known where the train was going. What if it didn't hit Charleston at all but went east into Virginia?

He spotted some shiny red berries and flew to them, wishing he'd paid closer attention when Jamie played science teacher. Were the white ones poison and you could often eat the red? Or was it the other way around?

He moved on, scouring the ground until he found a dried-up husk of green tomato. It had probably been part of the stationmaster's sandwich. With his beak, Bitty plucked out the four remaining tomato seeds. It wasn't much of a lunch. It wasn't even much of a snack. But it was something.

Satisfied that he wasn't going to starve, not this moment, at least, Bitty flew back to the depot roof. Back home, Jamie, with his sore hand, had probably gone to school, and the birds of the Big House had gone into the darkness of the mine. Bitty squinted in the sunshine. Already it seemed like another life.

Chapter 8

The thing about being bored when you're free, Bitty learned, is that you can actually do something about it. When he tired of the depot, he explored the bushes, keeping low in case he needed to make a quick escape. So far he hadn't seen Cipher or any of the hawk's brothers and sisters, who he imagined must be watching from the trees. But near a tangle of thorns he saw two jays and a robin—wild birds. Up close, they didn't look so different. The way Uncle Aubrey talked about them, Bitty had figured they'd be spitting and swearing.

He waved. They waved back.

He lifted his left foot. The robin lifted hers.

He lifted his right foot. The robin did the same.

The shorter of the two jays laughed. "Daft, ain't he?" he said. "Blonds."

"He's not daft, bub. You just scared him," said the other jay. "It's okay, bird, we ain't gonna hurt ya."

"Nah, look at him. He's slow. See how puny he is?"

Slow? Bitty? The only one of Jamie's birds who could spell *ornithological* without hesitating? Bitty tried to think of a snappy comeback, but saying he was "small-boned" didn't seem to cut it. He flew away instead.

"I'd really like to talk," he yelled back at them, so the birds would know that he *could* talk. "But I have someplace important to be."

Crash.

He hit an oak tree full-on and fell back into the soft moss that lay like a blanket beneath it.

"See?" said the jay. "Daft."

"I think he's hurt," said the robin. "Are you hurt?"

Bitty shook his head. The world steadied.

A squirrel scampered past him, then dashed toward a hollow tree, making a chattering noise that sounded as if he were blowing a raspberry.

That's rude, Bitty thought. The robin and jays must have thought so, too, because they scattered. Then Bitty felt, rather than saw, a shadow.

The hawk.

He searched for a place to hide and found another pricker bush. The roots made a small cave, and he squeezed himself inside.

Quiet as death, the hawk landed. There was no mistaking the wing. It was Cipher.

"Fee, fi, fo, fum," she said, tilting her head from one side to the other. "I can find you now or I can find you later. But I will find you. I've developed a taste for canary."

Bitty had never heard her speak so many words. Her voice was high and harsh. It seemed like hours before her wings lifted and she disappeared into a stand of virgin timber.

It wasn't until late afternoon, when Bitty heard the steam engine's whistle, that he dared to leave his hiding place. He was cramped from the cold, but he flew quickly, looking behind him so often he might as well have been flying backward. The brakes of the train screamed at him as he arrived at the depot. Up close, the train was a monster: big and black and snorting smoke that mixed with the March air. Men appeared as if from nowhere to stoke the glowing fire that rumbled in the engine's belly.

Bitty flew above the cars, which were overflowing with coal, until he found one where the coal dipped low, leaving a nice little seat, protected from the wind. He settled in and the waiting began again, this time for the train to pull away. The coal was more comfortable than he'd thought it would be. Bitty allowed his body to relax. By the time the locomotive belched and hissed into motion, he had closed his eyes. In minutes, he was asleep.

Tooooooooooooooooooooooooot.

The whistle sounded like a grieving owl. Bitty opened his eyes, half expecting to see the wire bars of the Big House and the walls of Jamie's bedroom. Instead, he saw a long streamer of smoke splitting the darkening sky.

He stretched—he was becoming fond of stretching—and smoothed the feathers that had been ruffled by the wind. He listened to the chug of the locomotive. Then he heard another sound, squeaky and high.

"You sure can sleep."

Bitty looked around the coal car. "Pardon?"

"I said you sure can sleep," the voice repeated. "Slumber. Drowse. You've been out for over an hour."

"When did you come on board?" Bitty asked the voice. There— that was the source: a small mouse, the light-gray color of morning. "And how did you learn to speak Bird?"

"From a bird, of course," the mouse said. He twitched his ears and sniffed. "A cardinal, actually. They're capital birds. Capital as in first class, but also capital as in they are the official state bird of West Virginia. A double meaning, you see. I also speak fluent Cat. And Mouse, but that's a given."

Bitty had never known any mice. There were a couple in the Campbells' house, but they hid under the floorboards and rarely ventured out. Bitty had never thought about striking up a conversation with one of them.

"Are you from Charleston?" he asked, assuming a mouse this cosmopolitan must be from a big city.

"I'm *going* to Charleston," said the mouse. "I'm originally from Red Springs, a small municipality but reputable nonetheless. My name is Eck, by the way. Pleased to make your acquaintance."

"Eck." Considering the mouse's sophisticated speech, Bitty had expected a high-society name, maybe something that ended with "the Third."

"It's short for Esquire," the mouse added.

"I'm Bitty."

"Is that short for anything?" Eck asked.

"No. It's just my name."

"Are you headed for Charleston?"

"You bet I am." Bitty craned his neck see what sort of scenery they might be passing. "How much did I miss? Is Charleston the only stop left?"

"It's not the only *stop* left," Eck said. "There are plenty of small towns, which are charming if you like that sort of thing. But Charleston is the only city worth stopping *at*. Or rather, the only city at which you should stop. *For* which you should stop? I need to study up on my Bird grammar. Of course, I'm better than I used to be. At first the only phrases I knew were 'Those are lovely petunias' and 'I'm lost,' which weren't very useful. I hate petunias. And I'm never lost."

"Your Bird is better than my Mouse," Bitty said. "I can't even say hello."

"I spent years studying," said Eck.

Suddenly, the canary wasn't sure he had all he needed to make it in the city.

"Are you okay?" Eck asked him. "You seem a bit adrift."

"I guess I am," Bitty admitted. "This is my first time on a train. This is my first time anywhere. Until this morning, I lived in a cage."

"A cage?" The mouse's eyes, which until now had looked somewhat beady, opened wide. "Were you a pet?"

"A coal miner," Bitty said. "But in my off hours there was a boy—"

"A miner?" Eck's voice grew higher and squeakier. "Were you one of the famous mining canaries? If so, I've heard all about you."

Bitty's beak opened. Living in a cage, he hadn't heard much about anyone else in the animal world, save the occasional news story about a brave dog. "Famous?"

"*You risk your lives to save the lives of men,*" Eck quoted, regaining control of his voice. "Am I right?" He looked at Bitty with new admiration. "I'm not sure I would have done it."

Bitty shrugged. "It's not like I had much choice. I was a prisoner."

"My third cousins were prisoners." Eck leaned forward. "Snake food."

Bitty shuddered. "Was that in Charleston?"

"No, it was much farther east. So *you* were the canary in the coal mine. We have mines near Charleston, but I don't think they use canaries anymore. Mechanization, you know. Not that it made much difference. It's the economy. No one's working. No one's eating. Is that why you're here? Did your mine shut down, too?"

"No," Bitty said. "I left."

"I see." Eck's voice squeaked with something—not disappointment, exactly, but Bitty felt compelled to explain.

"I'm here on a mission."

"Spy mission? Hush hush?"

"It's no secret," Bitty said. "Canaries are dying at the mine where I work—worked. People are dying, and getting hurt. And there's a lot more the company could be doing when things"—he swallowed and thought of Aunt Lou—"go wrong. Charleston is where they make laws, so I'm going to meet with the legislature. It's time to save the lives of canaries as well as the lives of men."

There. That sounded worthy. And it had the added benefit of being true.

"Have you gotten on their schedule yet?" Eck asked.

"Not yet," Bitty said. "I guess that's what I have to do first."

No, first he had to find someone who could speak Human. Perhaps the mouse—

"Do you speak Human?" Bitty asked, though he was sure Eck would have mentioned it if he did.

"I understand it, but I don't speak it, per se," the mouse said. "Not in a way they'd understand. It takes a willful fancy for a human to listen to a mouse. Most humans lack willful fancy. Especially those in politics. But you've probably figured out a way to get around all that."

Bitty hadn't figured out anything. But he would. He changed the subject. "What are *you* going to do in Charleston?" He'd never thought about mice going anywhere, besides back beneath the floorboards.

"I work in the Gilmer Inn, one of Charleston's finest hotels," Eck said. "My family has been employed there for three generations. We get plenty of important visitors—some of your legislators, in fact. The service is unequaled."

"Mice *work?*"

Eck stood up tall and let out an angry puff of breath. "Of course we work," he said. "Well, not all of us; there are a few layabouts. But any mouse worth his cheese has a job. Did you think you were the only ones who performed a valuable service?"

"I didn't mean to offend you," Bitty said. "I guess living in a cage, you don't learn enough about the world. Except for newspapers and Jamie's adventure stories, and those were mostly made up—"

At the word *cage*, Eck calmed down again. "No," he said. "I don't suppose you would learn very much in a cage. I have approximately sixty-seven miles left to educate you, so we'd better begin. Let's start with my family. Some of us are housekeepers. We keep the inn tidy, keep the crumbs off the floors. But I, personally, don't do housekeeping." He stood straight and tall again. "I," he said, "am an animal trainer."

"Like in the circus?"

"That would be show business," Eck said. "I'm in charge of the Gilmer Inn House Cats. You've heard of them, of course."

"I'm afraid not." Bitty found himself speaking more formally, to match the mouse's tone.

"Four cats reside at the Gilmer Inn," Eck said. "A formidable bunch. I keep them on a strict regimen. If it weren't for me, they'd spend their days just lying around, thinking. I usually work year-round, but I spent the winter down south. I hear the cats have grown rather rotund in my absence. Days in front of the fire. No pouncing. I'll have my work cut out for me."

It seemed to Bitty that the mouse would have been pleased to be around cats that didn't pounce, but a gleam in Eck's eye said otherwise. "Is it dangerous, being an animal trainer?" Bitty asked. The Campbells didn't have cats, but the Gap-Toothed Man and his wife did, a tigress named Kitty. She'd murdered the Gap-Toothed Man's own canary, which was why he'd started renting birds from Jamie. That was a part of Bitty's education that was already complete: he knew cats had claws; he knew what they ate for dinner.

"I suppose it could be dangerous, if you got caught," Eck said. "Nobody in my family has been caught for years. We do extensive physical training."

He made a mouse muscle, and the canary saw that he was in very good shape indeed. Bitty's own muscles were still sore from the day's flying. His head was clear, though. He felt as if he could see for miles. With a quick flutter, he reached the top of the coal car and stared into the distance, trying to keep his footing in the wind.

"What do you see?" shouted Eck, who was still below the wind line.

"Not much. It's so dark. And..." Bitty's voice left him. He had expected to be pressed on both sides by mountains, but instead, as his eyes adjusted, he saw that the landscape to the left of the train had fallen away, as if a monster had eaten a chunk of it.

Eck scrambled up next to Bitty, holding tight to the top of the train car.

"What is that?" Bitty whispered.

"The New River," Eck said reverently. "Soon it'll turn into the Kanawha."

"The Kana—"

"Ku-NAH-wuh. It's an Indian name." Eck's voice had a smile in it. "I suppose it does look frightening in the dark."

"Kanawha," Bitty echoed. In the moonlight, the water looked nearly black. The coal car—so much bigger than the bamboo carrier—rocked as they rounded a curve, but for once, his stomach didn't rock with it. He inhaled. He didn't have much of a sense of smell—few birds did—but even in the darkness he could tell that this part of West Virginia had a head start on spring. The trees seemed fuller here. Back home, the leaves were just beginning to unfurl. For once, Bitty felt he was a part of the world, even if he didn't know so much about it.

The train passed through woodland, other coal camps and a burning slag heap—the waste left after the coal had been mined and sorted. The houses seemed to get smaller and poorer until there were no houses at all, just a neighborhood of tents that made the Campbells look like millionaires. One family sat by a fire, but they weren't cooking over it. A baby wailed, her voice so sharp that Bitty heard it over the chugging of the train.

"Hard times," Eck intoned. "Someone once said: 'If you keep hope in your pocket you will lose it. It's best to keep hope in your heart.'"

"Who said that?"

"Well," Eck admitted, "I did. Cats are great philosophers, you know. Some of it was bound to rub off."

Bitty was about to ask Eck what philosophers said about hunger when he heard a noise that sounded like crunching.

"Mmph u loch shma?" the mouse asked.

"Hunh?" said Bitty, thinking it was another language.

"Mmph...Pardon me. Would you care for some?" repeated Eck. "It's peanut butter cracker. Not Gilmer Inn quality, but quite delicious. Ambrosial."

"Thank you," Bitty said, and took a small piece. It stuck to his beak. "Ish brumph." He swallowed. "Ambrosial."

It was a small cracker, as Eck was a small mouse. But the gnawing spot in Bitty's stomach was filled. He was sure he had never tasted anything this good, and it was only the thought of the little family by the fire that kept him from enjoying it fully.

Bitty and Eck chatted on as the mountains stood guard above them. Charleston lay ahead.

"*Montani Semper Liberi*," Eck quoted again. "That's Latin. State motto. 'Mountaineers Are Always Free.'"

"*Montani Semper Liberi*," Bitty repeated. He hadn't always been free, but he was free now. Stars dotted the sky above him. They disappeared as the train went through a tunnel; then they appeared again, and winked at him. Soon, the train arrived in the capital.

"That's the passenger station over there," Eck said as the train slowed just shy of a large two-story building with arched windows that glowed like the eyes of a jack-o'-lantern. "Neoclassical, very well designed. I get off at the freight station, but I think you'll find this one more to your liking. You'll find your legislators in the courthouse on my side of the river. Remember: it's the Gilmer Inn in the East End if you get into any trouble. And even if you don't."

The mouse gathered his belongings, which consisted of a second peanut butter cracker and a chunk of hard cheese. He stored them both in an empty tea bag. Then he strapped the bag over his shoulder like a satchel, and sat ready to disembark. Bitty had no belongings. He said his good-byes and was preparing to take flight when the mouse spoke again.

"One of our frequent guests at the inn is an inventor. The last time he was here, he said something about coal. Of course, he could have said 'bowl.' I was chasing one of the cats so I didn't hear it all, but I distinctly remember him saying his invention could send some canaries to the unemployment line. Or maybe he said 'fairies.' I *was* running at the time. At any rate, you should meet him."

The unemployment line sounded like a bad thing to the Campbells and to Uncle Aubrey, but to Bitty, it sounded like a solution.

"I'll come see him," Bitty agreed as the train started speeding up again. "And you. Thanks again for the cracker."

"Stop by after you visit your legislators," Eck called. "As a famous cat philosopher once said: 'Keep your claws sharp and your wits sharper.' And don't take any wooden nickels." He shook himself and his fur stood on end, as if he'd stuck his pink foot in an electrical socket, or had been frightened by the very cat he was quoting.

Bitty wanted to ask if a wooden nickel was like miners' scrip, but it was time to go. Ahead, the lights of the railway station glowed, and Bitty flew toward them. Late as it was, there were people everywhere. He had never felt so alone.

Chapter 9

Bitty flew to the Chesapeake & Ohio station on heavy wings. He landed on a stone railing that bordered the second-floor balcony. The station was shorter than a coal tipple but taller than the buildings back home. The roof reminded him of Mrs. Campbell's flowerpots. Through the windows he could see marble floors and a spiral staircase. And down below? People. Only about two hundred people lived in Coalbank Hollow proper, and right now, every one of them would likely be asleep, preparing for an early morning. It seemed as if there were half that many people at the train station, streaming in and out of the lobby and calling to one another in the artificial light.

Bitty flew around the building once to get his bearings. Just across the tracks, he could make out a trail leading up the mountain. Beside it, catching the moon like a mirror, he saw a creek, with a small waterfall, flowing through last year's leaves. The sound of the rushing water seemed gentle enough, but Bitty landed close to the trail, where the water moved more slowly. He lit on a rock and leaned over to take a few sips, aware of the strange moaning sounds the trees made. He took a few more sips and froze. Was someone watching him, or was he just not used to the noises here? One more sip, to pretend he wasn't afraid, and then he zipped back to the light of the train station.

He found a nook on the balcony where he couldn't be seen by passengers or by the snarling, winged lions' heads that decorated the building. He heard a strange cooing sound coming from somewhere above him. It wasn't a scary sound, but he thought it better to stay hidden than to investigate. From his hiding place, he counted people until his breathing returned to normal. Every one of those people had a destination. Bitty had reached his. In the morning, his friends would go back to work in the mines. Bitty would go to work aboveground, to try to help them.

Again, it was a train whistle that woke him. Bitty stretched his wings, stiff from the cold. The sun was shining, but its rays hadn't yet reached the river, which was no longer a black snake but a white one. Fog rose from the water, the way steam rises from soup. Bitty knew he'd have to approach it—would have to cross it, to get to the legislators and to get to Eck—but first he returned to the small creek behind the station.

He found a sturdy rock for his perch and bent low to drink. At home, there would be a line behind him. Here, there was no one. Bitty drank without stopping. He finally paused and looked at his reflection in the water. An older bird stared back. Not just a little older; ancient. Bitty's feathers were no longer yellow, but gray. Had his escape aged him that much? He *had* been sleeping an awful lot, but he remembered his aunt Lou, a confirmed insomniac, telling him once: "Sleep is for the young."

Then he realized: the coal dust! He'd been sitting on the train for hours in a nest of coal and silt. He ducked his head into the cold water, then rubbed his face against his wing. He looked back at his reflection and saw his bright colors returning.

I'm not a miner anymore, he thought. Besides, he'd need to look his best if he was going to start hobnobbing with politicians. He began to scrub in earnest. The water was icy, but clean. It was important, he knew, to be near a good water supply. It would be nice living by the little creek, with the trail, and the protection of the mountain. Before Bitty could picture how nice it would be, something dark blocked out the sun. It torpedoed toward him, fast and heavy.

Bitty didn't wait to figure out what it was. He dove into the creek, where it still felt like winter. Just as he went under, the dark thing changed direction and headed back toward the sky. Sputtering, Bitty climbed back to his dry rock.

The dark thing came at him again. It laughed like Mr. Stinson, one of the Campbells' former boarders, when he drank the wrong kind of liquor.

Bitty dropped back into the water. The cold made his legs hurt. The rest of his body felt numb. He surfaced to breathe. The black thing was nowhere in sight.

"Hey," Bitty told the air. "W-w-w-watch it." He thought he sounded reasonably brave, despite the quaver in his voice.

"Watch it." A voice came back at him from the trees, flat and nasal. "Watch it. Watch it."

The black thing hurtled toward him again. This time, it landed on the rock and leaned down. Bitty found himself staring into a pair of cruel yellow eyes. A grackle. At least they weren't the red eyes of a hawk. Bitty had seen grackles through the window at home, packs of them in pine trees. This one seemed to be alone. Bitty found another rock a few feet away and rested there.

Another grackle missile hurtled toward him. "*Chck. Chck.* Watch it. Watch it," the bird cackled. Suddenly, the air seemed full of grackles, all shouting in the same mocking tone: "Watch it. Watch it." Black grackle beaks were everywhere, and feathers, dark as coal. They swarmed around him like bees. They whirled around him like a tornado. Bitty buried his head in his chest and shut his eyes. He was trapped, just the way he'd been trapped at the mine.

And then, from somewhere beneath the shrieks and laughter, he heard a friendly voice.

"Hey!" it hollered. "Canary. Over here."

Bitty raised his head as a grackle's claw grazed him.

"Over here!" the voice shouted again. Bitty tried to wipe the last of the creek water from his eyes as he flew, blindly, toward the voice. He could feel the heat of the grackles' breath behind him. He could hear the snap of their beaks.

"Hurry up! You're almost here."

"I'm... coming." It was hard to get the words out. He angled his wings and zoomed low, following the voice. Finally, he skidded to a halt.

Bitty wiped his eyes again and found himself underneath a green bench. Sitting on the bench was a man. At first Bitty thought it was the man who had called to him. Then he saw a group of birds huddled around one of the bench's metal supports.

"You made it!" said the bird who'd done the yelling. Mrs. Campbell would have called him husky; Uncle Aubrey would have said he was fat. "Don't worry. You'll be safe here."

For a moment, Bitty could only shake the water from his feathers and breathe, his heart pounding in his ears. The bird seemed to understand, and waited. The other birds, who were just as plump as the first one, stayed in their cluster, making strange cooing sounds that Bitty recognized from the night before. Above them, a last grackle dive-bombed the bench.

The old man stood up. He raised a long wooden cane into the air like a magician. "*Git!*" he yelled. "Go on. *Git.*" The grackles retreated into the trees.

"Thank you!" Bitty shouted to the man, who sat down again without hearing. Bitty turned to the birds. "Thanks," he said. "I thought I was a goner."

"Aw, that's their idea of fun," said the bird who'd saved him. "V and the Boys have never actually *killed* anybody. At least, I don't think they have."

"They're hoodlums, that's what they are," said another bird, whose head wobbled as if it were attached to a spring. Her voice wobbled with it. "Imagine, picking on a little guy like you."

Bitty was so relieved to be out of danger that he didn't even bristle at being called a little guy. "What does V stand for?"

"Viper," said the first bird.

"Sorry I asked."

"I'm Clarence," said the bird. "This is my mom, Eudora." Eudora nodded (or perhaps she had just never stopped nodding). "And this is Roger, Pyro, Georgia and T-Baby."

Bitty's new friends were dull gray, with the exception of their

45

necks, which shimmered purple and blue, as if they were some kind of royalty. Their stomachs reminded him of some of the miners – the old-timers, whose working days were behind them and who never seemed to move except to take a sip from a soda bottle.

Overhead, there was a rattling noise, and the birds left the safety of the bench and clustered around the old man's feet. "Come on," Clarence said, giving Bitty a nudge. "Breakfast."

Breakfast turned out to be crusts of hard white bread and flakes of cracker that fell like snow from the old man's wrinkled hands. Bitty had never seen so much food.

"All this is for you?" he asked. "And you don't even have to wait in a breadline?" Bitty had never seen a breadline, but he'd read about them.

Clarence nodded, his mouth full. "You should have seen us *before* the depression," he said when he swallowed. "Loaves of bread. Now all we get is the crusts."

"And remember when his wife used to make us that burnt sugar cake?" Clarence's mother sighed. "But we're very lucky. We eat."

Bitty ate his share of breakfast (the peanut butter cracker seemed long ago), and when he was finished, it was as if he'd never been hungry.

"Here," the old man said, rising and sprinkling some bread off to the side so the grackles could get at it. "But mind, you chase that wee bird any more and it'll be your last supper." He winked at Bitty and his new friends, who cooed their thanks. Bitty gave a low whistle.

"You guys sure have it easy."

"Says you." Clarence's feathers were clearly ruffled. "You think our life is all bread and crackers?" The other birds stopped cooing.

A gnawing feeling that wasn't hunger settled in Bitty's stomach. "I'm sorry," he said. "It's just that... well, this is my first week out of a cage." The word *cage* worked the same magic it had worked with Eck.

"Aw, that's okay," Clarence said, relaxing. "I don't mean to get touchy. But everyone always thinks the worst of us. I'm just looking out for our reputation."

"What are you, exactly? I've never seen a bird like you before."

"Me?" Clarence said. "Well, I'm...we're pigeons. Don't tell me you've never heard of pigeons?"

Bitty took a step backward. "Lazy good-for-nothings." That was what his uncle Aubrey called pigeons. "Scavengers. Rats with wings. Carry diseases. Never done an honest day's work in their lives."

"Yup," Clarence said. "You've heard of us."

Clarence didn't look as if he was carrying any diseases. Still. Bitty took another step back.

"Aw, don't tell me you believe all the stereotypes." The pigeon jerked his head to the side, warding off an imaginary punch.

Bitty stopped moving. He'd flown from the robin and the jays. He'd flown from the grackles. The pigeons had saved him. They looked perfectly healthy. And Uncle Aubrey wasn't right about everything. Maybe it was time to stop flying away.

"We know what you've heard," Clarence said, and the others bobbed their heads. "We're a bunch of bums, right? Lazy, right?"

"That's some of it," Bitty admitted.

"Well, it's not true," Clarence said. "Not one word."

"We're company birds," said Clarence's brother—T-Baby, Bitty thought it was.

"Oh," said Bitty, who didn't understand at all. He thought about the company men back home, the ones who made decisions "for the good of the mine" but not necessarily for the good of the workers. Jamie's father didn't have much nice to say about company men.

"Company birds," Clarence repeated. "That means we...Well, come on, I'll just show you."

Clarence flew to another bench, and Bitty followed him, catching up quickly because Clarence's flying was slow and went in fits and starts.

"See her?" Clarence asked, nodding toward an old woman who didn't move, except for her hands, which folded and unfolded a pale blue handkerchief. "That's Mrs. Gillespie. Her son hasn't written her in more than a month *and* she has arthritis."

They flew to another bench. "Mr. Oznowicz," Clarence said. "He used to work for a five-and-dime, but people aren't buying as much as they used to so he got canned. His wife says he needs a hobby so she sends him here to feed us."

At the next bench, a man with a droopy face and the biggest feet Bitty had ever seen grinned at them.

"Hobo Pete," Clarence said. "He sleeps here."

"You sure know a lot of humans," Bitty said, thinking of his own humans in Coalbank Hollow.

"We know 'em all," Clarence said. "It's our job to keep them company. We nod a lot, make them feel like someone's listening. They feed us. It makes them happy to see us eat. They protect us like Mr. Stanley back there, and we make sure nobody messes with them, either." He put up his wings, bobbing and weaving as if he were in a boxing ring.

"*Company* birds!" The lightbulb finally went on in Bitty's brain. "You keep people *company*."

"That's what I've been telling you," Clarence said. "There are lots of lonely humans out there. And I mean *lots*. If we don't eat what they feed us, they don't feel appreciated. It's not so easy, eating all the time. That was the fifth breakfast I've had this morning."

"Do other birds have work, too?" Bitty asked. The robin and jays hadn't looked especially busy, nor had the turkey vultures he'd watched sailing the ridge back home.

"Of course they do," Clarence said. "We're in construction, cleaning, show biz—if you've got some free time, I can introduce you around. You being fresh out of a cage and all."

"That'd be great," Bitty said. "I'm not sure how much time I'll have. Actually, I'm here on a mission." He told Clarence about the mine and the dangers there, which the company often ignored. Canaries—even good canaries, like Boggs—were easy to replace. So were men.

"When Mr. Polly died, do you know what they told his wife?" Bitty said. " 'Let us know if you need an extra week or two to pay off your debt.' And they thought they were being generous. At least she had the other miners to take her in and help her out."

Clarence nodded, and Bitty could see how the pigeon had gotten a job as a professional listener. "Why did you finally leave?" Clarence asked.

Bitty tried to explain. "I was saving my own tail feathers, that was part of it," he said. "And I want to save my friends." That was the rest.

He told Clarence about little Sammy Sowers, too, the kid who got chocolate from the legislature just because he asked for it.

"So that's why I'm here. To ask."

"You're going to ask the state government for a bar of chocolate?" Clarence said, but Bitty could see he was teasing.

"Nope. I'm going to ask for the moon," Bitty said.

"Listen, I've got to get to work," Clarence told him. "But if you need a place to spend the night, meet us on the roof. There's safety in numbers, and that's where we sleep."

"I've got to get to work, too," Bitty said. "I'll find you later. Thanks again." He flapped his wings and soared skyward. Then he turned and faced the river.

Chapter 10

Bitty lit on a beam of the bridge that spanned the Kanawha. The fog had lifted, and he could see the water, a muddy green, rushing over the rocks below. He didn't want to estimate the drop. He openly admitted that he got sick to his stomach anytime someone swung him around in a cage, but he was slower to own up to his nagging fear of heights.

He had to cross. In the distance, he could see the new capitol, its great dome perched upon it like a derby. Somewhere over the river, he would find the courthouse, where the legislators were meeting until the new building was complete. He should have asked Clarence for directions. But he was sure someone would help him once he got to the other side.

Part of him wanted to find Eck first, to find out whether the inventor had booked his usual room at the Gilmer Inn. And the truth was, he wanted to see a familiar face. But it was the politicians he needed to study if he was going to follow through with his plan.

He hesitated, listening to the river. Then he took a deep breath and flapped his way across, staying just above the bridge so he was never flying over the open water. He kept his eyes on the buildings in the distance.

At last, he reached the other side. He found a farmers' market where jars of jelly were stacked high, the sun lighting them up like jewels. The market had fresh bread and fried sweet potato pies. A few people let the golden flakes from those pies fall to the ground. Bitty tried to grab them, but a group of sparrows got there first. It was just as well; he'd eaten plenty and there was someplace he needed to be. Boggs and Mr. Polly had been dead for thirty-seven days. The mine's record for days without an accident was 103. That gave Bitty just sixty-six days, at most. According to Uncle Aubrey, the government moved at a snail's pace, not a bird's. Bitty imagined Chester and Alice in the darkness of the mine, the Gap-Toothed Man feeding Aunt Lou a hard chunk of biscuit. It was time for action.

Apparently, everyone on the north side of the river felt the same way. As he flew along, Bitty saw men rushing up and down the steps of tall buildings, their shoes tapping. A streetcar hurried down the track and Bitty flew to the side to get out of its way. Women's dresses bloomed like flower gardens. Bitty thought of Mrs. Campbell's dresses, the patterns so faded you couldn't tell they'd been flowers at all.

He passed the theater, dark by day. He passed men, their hands held out for a dime. He passed birds, too, every one of whom seemed to have someplace important to go. Bitty cleared his throat. If he was going to be brave enough to present his case to the government, he would have to be brave enough to ask one of them for directions.

Just then, another shadow darkened the sky above him.

V and the Boys, he thought. He looked up, expecting to see the grackles' yellow eyes. Instead, he saw the curved beak of a hawk. He increased his speed and glanced upward again, taking a split second to check the wing and—it couldn't be. But there was no mistaking its shape. Cipher had followed him.

Bitty made a low dive, flapping his wings like a hummingbird. The hawk pierced the sky behind him. Bitty had a head start, but he didn't have the hawk's speed; there was no way to outfly her. In an alley below, he spotted a garbage can with the lid slightly ajar and homed in for a landing. It was a soft one. He slipped beneath the metal lid and was immediately coated in cinders and carrot scrapings.

"Fee, fi, fo, fum." Cipher's voice seemed to be coming from all sides. She hadn't improved her vocabulary since the last time they'd met.

Bitty froze and waited. Silence, then footsteps and a crunching sound. The whole can rattled and he felt himself being lifted into the air. Bitty knew hawks were strong, but this was like something out of the "Ripley's Believe It or Not!" column in the Charleston paper.

The can tipped. The canary tumbled, round head over pointy feet, in a waterfall of garbage. But instead of landing on the ground in the alley, Bitty found himself inside a large covered truck. The engine burbled. The horn beeped—*arrruuugah!*—and he was swept away from all he knew of his new city. He managed to peek through the crack at the back of the truck in time to see the hawk fly off with a limp rat, a consolation prize.

The truck turned. Bitty fell back into the garbage, the carrot peels wet against his wings. Right turn, left turn, right turn. His stomach churned and he tasted sour bread. One mile. More. Finally, the truck stopped. The whole back seemed to rise, and Bitty slid into a pile of everything that was curdled and rotten. The truck spun away, belching exhaust, but that was preferable to the other aroma, which was so strong that even Bitty, with his limited sense of smell, was aware of it. It was just a shade less pungent than the smell of death.

The garbage rose into small mountains. Bitty would have gagged, but he was so glad to be out of the truck and away from the hawk that he just burped once instead. And he had company. Birds, mostly white, but with storm-gray wings that made it look as if they were wearing jackets, filled the air. They were carrying trash from one pile to another and they were yelling at the top of their lungs.

"Tires!" one of them shouted. "Blasted automobiles. What do they expect us to do with these? Can't eat tires. Can't even move 'em."

"Glass," said another, in a voice that fell somewhere between a sob and a laugh. "Who needs it?"

And then: "Sardines. Gladys, come quick, sardines."

For all their complaining, the birds seemed to enjoy their work, and Bitty watched them drag shiny pieces of metal and soggy banana peels from pile to pile. They flew with such confidence that Bitty had no fear until he realized he had absolutely no idea where he was.

The train station seemed far away, the mines and his friends even farther. The clock was ticking. The chance to do something was ticking away with it. The only thing he seemed capable of doing was getting lost.

"Sir?" he called to a bird, who had a rubber boot in his mouth and didn't answer.

"Ma'am?" he called to the bird named Gladys.

She hovered in the air above him, as if she were attached to a string. "Look at you, so polite! What can I do for you?"

"I'm Bitty," he began.

"Now, *that* I can't do anything about."

"No, I mean my *name* is Bitty," he said. "And I'm kind of . . . that is, I'm really . . . I'm lost." As soon he uttered the word, he stopped talking. He wasn't sure whether it was tears or garbage that caused his eyes to sting.

"Pickles to fiddlesticks," Gladys said. "You can't be lost. You're with me, and I'm not lost. Hey, Phil!"

The bird with the sardines flew over. "This one says he's lost," Gladys said.

"How can that be? He's with us; we're not lost," Phil said.

"Exactly what I told him."

"If I'm not lost, then where am I?" Bitty asked.

"You," said Phil, "are at the finest dining establishment in all of Kanawha County, which just happens to be my place of employ."

"But where—"

"The dump, kid," said Phil. "You're at the dump."

"But isn't that—"

"Garbage," Phil said. "Beautiful, isn't it? Our little slice of heaven."

"We came here on our very first date," Gladys said.

"Smoked oysters," added Phil. "I'd been saving them for someone special. And then this vision of loveliness—"

"Oh, Phil, stop!"

"I get carried away," Phil said. "There are worse things, am I right? So you're lost. Where are you trying to get, kid? Back to the pet store?"

"To the courthouse," Bitty said. "I'm planning to meet with some politicians."

"Dressed like that?" Phil asked. "Not that I worry much about fashion, you understand, but last time I checked, our esteemed representatives did not wear carrot peels to work. Not to mention—"

"Not to mention what?"

"I may not have the keenest olfactory sense, but you smell, kid."

"Phil," Gladys said.

"I speak the truth. I don't mean to be offensive, but you only get one chance to make a first impression."

The bird had a point. Bitty couldn't go before the legislators smelling like garbage, even if the garbage was relatively fresh.

Eck, then. The mouse would understand about the smell, and maybe even help him find a place to clean up.

"Then I need to get to the Gilmer Inn in the East End, please," Bitty said.

"What do you want with them?" said Phil. "Hoity-toity, that's what they are over there. You want a good time, you stick with us. This is living!"

"Phil," Gladys said. "I think he knows where he wants to go." She turned to Bitty. "Don't you worry, we know all about the Gilmer Inn. Look, right over there. That's their garbage. We don't get as much of it as we used to, but I'll say this for them: they make a terrific corn bread."

"Hoity-toity corn bread," Phil muttered.

Bitty moved closer to the small pile. He saw kitchen trash and sharp glass, and near that, some broken tubes and pieces of copper that had been fused together in a miniature dome. There was a flat piece, too, and painted across it, in a thin black brushstroke, was:

Whatchamacallit. G.D. No. 43159.

The inventor! Bitty thought. This must be *his* garbage. But why would he be throwing a perfectly good invention away? Unless... unless it wasn't perfectly good.

"You don't want to go to that inn," Phil said.

"Yes," Bitty said, "I do." He tugged at a wire. "Listen, do you know what my job was up until yesterday?"

"You were a movie star?" suggested Gladys.

"I was a coal miner," Bitty said.

"No offense, kid," said Phil, "but you don't look big enough to handle a shovel."

"I didn't *dig* the coal," Bitty explained. "I breathed it."

He told the birds about life underground, sniffing for gas instead of for garbage. He told them how safety lamps had been replacing birds in mines for years, but how the flame from one had caused an explosion in his mine—one big enough to make newspaper headlines. The men were reluctant to give up their birds, and even the canaries—well, Uncle Aubrey, anyway—didn't blame them.

" 'You'll never find a piece of mining equipment that's more sensitive than me.' That's what my uncle always says," Bitty continued. "Even if it's true, times are changing. They act like we're still in the 1800s."

"Sounds like a tough life, kid," said Phil. "I don't think I could survive in a cage, not with these wings. But what does all that have to do with the Gilmer Inn? I'm not following."

Bitty gave him the short version of the story but highlighted his chance meeting on the train with Eck, who'd told him about the inventor in the inn's smallest room. "I have to follow up every lead," he said.

"And this is a lead, am I right?" Gladys asked, indicating the dented copper and broken tubes.

"I think so."

"Kid knows what he's talking about," Phil said. Bitty didn't feel that way, but he was glad he at least gave the appearance of being in control. It gave him hope.

"Everything happens for a reason," Gladys said. "You meeting that mouse was no accident."

The word *accident* echoed in his brain. "So will you help me get to the inn?"

"Of course we will," Gladys said. She looked at Phil. "Do you know how to get to the inn?"

"Er," Phil said, "not exactly. Do you?"

"How would I? You've never taken me to the inn."

"Maybe if you had a map?" Bitty suggested.

"Attaboy, that's using your head!" Phil said. "No map. But don't worry. I've got something better."

He whistled loudly, and another bird appeared. This one had long, arched wings the color of one of the Gap-Toothed Man's cigars. Bitty had gotten to see those cigars up close on their walks together. Mine safety rules meant the cigar was never lit, so he never had to endure the stench of it.

"Hey, sugar," the bird said. Her accent was so different from the gulls' that at first Bitty thought she was speaking Squirrel. Or French. "What's a little thing like you doing all the way out here?"

"He's lost, obviously," Phil said. "He's trying to get to the Gilmer Inn in the East End." He turned to Bitty. "Dolly here's a chimney swift. Been in every chimney in Charleston."

"Well, not every chimney," Dolly said. "But I know that one. I'll get you where you need to go."

"And step on it," Phil said. "This kid's a coal miner. He's got important work to do. *Lives* are at stake."

Chapter 11

Bitty thanked Phil and Gladys and flew off with the swift. He stayed to her right, hoping to keep the aroma of the garbage, which clung to his feathers, downwind. She slowed her pace to match his.

"So what did Phil mean, 'lives are at stake'?" she asked.

Bitty recounted his tale briefly. It was good practice for when he figured out a way to make the lawmakers hear him. And the swift seemed interested, especially in the parts about safety, a subject on which she was an expert.

"I *thought* you were from out of town," she said. "We don't get many of your kind in the city, unless they're in cages."

"I lived in a cage," Bitty said. "But I'm free now."

As they flew, Dolly told him about the city—which buildings were safest and which he should avoid. The inn had received a first-class safety rating. "Too many cats for my taste," the swift said. "But the chimneys are perfect. No downdrafts."

"My friend works with those cats," Bitty said.

"Imagine inviting that sort of danger. Though there's danger everywhere, I suppose."

"I've seen it." Bitty told her about the grackles and the hawk.

"Those grackles," Dolly said. "They're ruining our reputation for down-home hospitality. And the hawks—"

"I didn't think hawks even lived in cities," Bitty said.

"We don't have many of them, mind, but we have a few. Two are nesting in the bell tower of the church, so be careful if that's on your route. I hear a third hawk moved in just this morning."

Bitty swallowed. Thankfully, the swift changed the subject. "So when did you leave your cage, honey?"

"Just yesterday," Bitty said. "I came here all the way from Coalbank Hollow."

"On those little wings?"

"I cheated," Bitty said. "I took the train most of the way. I'm staying at the station on MacCorkle Avenue."

The swift laughed. "That's not cheating, sweetheart, that's old-fashioned ingenuity. And that," she said, "is the East End."

Bitty recognized the farmers' market and was glad that something, at least, looked familiar. "There's Quarrier Street," said the swift as she flew on. "There's Virginia. And there"—she nodded—"is your Gilmer Inn."

"Thank you!" he shouted—more loudly than he needed to, as the swift was still beside him. "If there's ever anything I can do for you..."

"Well, shoot," she said. "I'm proud to help your cause. We all are. If you need anything, you just let me know." She gave him a peck on the cheek and disappeared into the chimney of the house next door, humming a melody from a song about blood and coal.

The Gilmer Inn stood back just a bit from the main road, though it was close to the houses on either side of it. It was huge—bigger than the houses he'd imagined the coal barons would own, with a lawn that looked as if the gardener must have cut it with a ruler and scissors. The houses beside it were big, too, with roofs that sloped down sharply, like wedges of cheese. But the inn stood out, in part because of the magnolia tree, budding pink in the front yard.

The houses in the East End were cleaner than the houses in the coal camp. They seemed untouched by poverty, at least from a distance. But as Bitty got closer, he saw peeling paint on some of the shutters. The hotel was marked by a brown sign with swirling letters. The building itself was made not of brick, like the surrounding houses, but of stucco and dark wood. On the top floor, there was a crisscross design, as if someone had started a giant game of tic-tac-toe but hadn't finished it. It made the inn seem as if it belonged far away—in England or Switzerland, perhaps, though the closest Bitty had gotten to any foreign country was the sound of the accents that sometimes blasted from the Campbells' radio. The inn was three stories high. How would he find Eck?

He circled twice and was about to take a third spin around when he spotted a cement pedestal topped by a large dish. A birdbath! There wasn't much water in it, but Bitty did what he could to wash away at least some of the smell of the dump. He couldn't get rid of all of it—he'd need the creek for that—but at least he'd be a little more respectable for a trip inside the inn. If he could get inside.

An upstairs window was open, but he didn't trust it. He remembered Eck describing a tunnel, an entrance to the basement near the back porch. On his first pass, he didn't see anything but a drainpipe and a large boulder. But on his second pass, he saw it: a potato-shaped hole just a foot or so away from the hotel, partially hidden by a gardenia bush that had not yet bloomed. Bitty worried that it could be a snake hole, and he remembered the fate of Eck's unfortunate cousins. But Eck would have warned him about a snake hole if he knew about it. And anyway, the snakes would still be hibernating. At least, that was what Bitty told himself.

"Helllooooo," he hollered into the hole.

No answer.

"Helllooooooo," he yelled again. There was no answer this time, either. Boldly, he headed into the darkness.

Chapter 12

Bitty could feel, but not see, the cool dirt walls as he worked his way down the passage. The temperature dropped, reminding him of the mines, where it stayed cold and damp year-round. That was bad for the canaries, who were susceptible to colds. Without proper care, a canary could die from a cold, but there were so many things in Bitty's life that could have killed him, he hadn't dwelled on it much. He remembered the ache from the last time he'd been sick; he remembered wanting to be warm. "What's wrong, Big Yellow?" Jamie had asked when he saw the canary shivering. He'd consulted his manual. (It was a point of pride with Uncle Aubrey that canaries were important enough to warrant manuals.) And Bitty had spent the next three days near the lamp by Jamie's bed. He remembered eating something called germicide, which tasted even worse than it sounded. On the fourth day, he went back to the main cage and the ache was gone.

The light at the end of the dirt tunnel brought Bitty back to the present. Cautiously, he stepped out and found himself in a large room lined with jars of peaches and beans and bottles of—was that wine? Prohibition made it illegal to make and sell alcohol—though that hadn't stopped the miners, as Bitty knew from Mr. Stinson. He supposed it didn't stop them in the Charleston, either. There was a whole row of the bottles, each bottle in its own little compartment. Braids of garlic hung from the ceiling. And on the floor, scurrying this way and that so that the room looked as busy as any city square, were dozens and dozens of mice.

"Ahem." Bitty cleared his throat. A few mice looked up at him, though none of them stopped moving to do so and there was a collision. An indignant mouse stood up, rubbing his head.

"You'd better have a good reason for being here," he squeaked in perfect Bird. "You aren't authorized. No one is."

"I'm looking for Eck," Bitty said.

"I don't know any Eck. Does anyone here know an Eck?" The mice shook their heads and shrugged their tiny shoulders.

"No Eck," said the angry mouse.

"I'm sorry to intrude," Bitty said. "I can see that you're busy." (Though what they were busy doing he wasn't sure.) "Eck should have gotten in late last night. Eck. Short for Esquire. He's an animal trainer."

"Oh, an animal trainer," the mouse said. The title seemed to carry some weight. "If he's *really* an animal trainer, he's upstairs in the main house on the first floor. You came into the cellar. They only send the cats down here at night."

"Could you direct me to the—" Bitty began.

"Back in the hole, first left. It's a steady climb up, then the third opening on your right."

"Got it," Bitty said. By the time he added a "thank you," the mouse had already gone back to whatever it was he was doing, but Bitty could feel the beady eyes upon him as he backed into the tunnel and began his upward climb.

It was slow going. He tried to use his wings, but the tunnel was so cramped that more often than not they were pinned to his sides. The dampness made him worry about getting sick. What would he do without Jamie to take care of him?

Bitty plodded on, and the path grew wider and more level. He saw a small hole to his right. One. Two. There it was. Bitty pushed his way through and found himself in a large room with a roaring fire. Above the fire was the head of a deer—no body, just the head, with antlers that spread toward the ceiling like the branches of a tree. Bitty nodded politely, though he knew the deer was dead and stuffed. But crouched down in front of the fire, looking very much alive, was a fat orange cat. And underneath a regal leather chair, only inches from the cat, was Eck.

"*Squeeeeeeeem*," Bitty heard Eck say, though he didn't know if his friend was speaking in Cat or Mouse. "*Squeeeeem*." Whatever it was, the cat understood. His ears twitched and he arched his back. Even so, Bitty could see the cat's ample stomach. Eck had his work cut out for him, all right. Still, the cat was quick.

"*Squeeeeem*," Eck said again. The cat pounced, reaching a long paw under the chair. That paw! Bitty hadn't had any idea a cat could stretch so far. Eck retreated, but only a few steps.

"I hope he knows what he's doing," Bitty muttered.

"*Squeeeeem*." This time the sound didn't come from Eck, and Bitty followed the noise across the room to another hole in the wall, where he saw another mouse about Eck's size staring the cat in the eye. Quickly, the cat bounded across the room and reached his paw into the hole. As soon as the cat moved, Eck started running toward the hole that Bitty had just popped out of. And as soon as he started running, the cat changed direction. He bounded toward Eck and, consequently, toward Bitty.

"Go, go, go, go, go!" Eck yelled, and Bitty dove into the hole. He felt a push on his rump and then another, and finally he was back in the damp darkness, with the mouse right behind him.

"Keep going!" Eck shouted in Bird. "*Run!*"

Bitty, who wasn't very graceful when it came to running, hurled his body forward until at last Eck yelled: "*Stop! It's all right; we can stop now.*"

Bitty looked back toward the light just as the cat's paw came shooting toward him, claws extended like switchblades.

"*Reow. Merow.*" The paw came to a stop three inches short of where they stood.

"*Eow. Mrrph,*" Eck replied. He turned to Bitty, breathing hard.

"Don't worry, we're safe. That was enough of a workout for one morning, I suppose. Come on, follow me."

"What was he saying back there?"

"Oh, that," Eck said. "'*Retraite.*' French, you know, it's a fencing term. He also said he was hungry for mouse pâté."

"And what did you say?"

"I said, 'Until next time, foolish feline.'"

Bitty was glad to see they were coming to another opening, a warmer spot inside the wall but close to the fireplace. Another mouse joined them, and Bitty recognized her as the mouse from across the room.

"Bonnie, my partner," Eck said. "Meet Bitty, formerly of Coalbank Hollow."

"The miner bird?"

"None other. Only his second day out of a cage."

"Second day out," Bonnie repeated. "And you've already faced a cat."

"And grackles. And a hawk. And, uh, garbage." Bitty told his story, pleased that they gasped in all the right places and that neither of them said anything about the way he smelled. "I think the new hawk's from Coalbank Hollow, too," he concluded. "She has a taste for canary."

"Well, she didn't get you, did she?" Bonnie said. Her smile was as warm as toast and made Bitty think of Alice. "You're a real adventurer."

"*You're* the adventurers, dealing with those cats every day," Bitty said. "Not me."

"An adventure," said Eck, "is an exciting or dangerous undertaking. By my count, you've had nothing but adventures for the past two days, if not for your entire life. Since birth."

Bitty found it hard to believe that an adventure could happen to someone who lived in a cage, to someone whose wings ached after only twenty minutes of flying. But what Eck said was true. He began to wish that he hadn't washed his face in the creek or the birdbath; that he'd left it coated with the dust and aromas of worldly experience, even if one of those worldly experiences happened to be garbage. He'd be sure not to bathe as quickly when he returned to Coalbank Hollow.

"So is he here?" Bitty asked. "The inventor?"

Bonnie looked at Eck, who nodded. "He has his usual room at the end of the hall," Eck said. "It's rarely occupied, as there aren't as many people traveling these days who can afford hotels. I think Miss Alma lets him have it for free. He's her first cousin, only once removed."

"Can we visit him?" Bitty asked. He didn't know much about science, but he thought he'd be able to tell right away if the man could help him—could help all of them.

"Naturally."

Bitty and Eck left Bonnie and hurried down the passageway, stopping now and then to peep through a mouse hole into what Eck promised were the inn's more interesting chambers.

They visited the bathroom first, with its inside plumbing and a tub that stood on lion's paws. "A claw-foot," Eck said. "It reminds Miss Alma of the cats." They admired the inn's radio, arched and curved like a church window, though it was silent. In the Campbells' house, the radio was often on, whether it was music—Aunt Lou loved to hear the Carter Family sing about hard times—or President Hoover talking in his clipped auctioneer's monotone about his latest plan to end those hard times. Whatever the plan, Mr. Campbell always said, it wasn't enough.

Finally, they reached the room at the end of the hall that was smaller than the rest. On the floor was a rug, depicting a peacock in its blue-green glory. Bitty and Eck stepped out of the hole. There was nobody there. A suitcase sat latched on a stand at the foot of the bed. Boldly, Bitty took a few more steps away from the mouse hole. His feet touched the carpet, and he might have stayed there, surrounded by the softness, if he hadn't seen, on a table above him, an instrument surrounded by a jumble of wires, copper and tubes.

He flew to the table and landed, the wires surrounding his legs like tentacles. Eck moved toward the table, too, but did not climb beyond its base.

"Well?" Eck said. "What do you think? Is it the solution?"

"Hard to say," Bitty said. "Wait a minute. I think these are notes."

The notes were beneath the object, so he couldn't see all the diagrams. The writing was much harder to read than the newsprint Bitty was used to. He made out the word *gas,* and *revolutionary* and most important of all, *miners.* And then he spotted, at the bottom of the page, a rough sketch of a bird that looked a little like him.

Focusing his eyes as best he could, he tried to wade through a dense paragraph that was labeled *Whatchamacallit.*

"As canaries stop singing when gas is identified in mines, thus requiring constant monitoring, this mechanism will behave in the opposite way, featuring an alarm system that will 'chirp' loudly when too much gas encroaches upon breathable air." There were other words written on the page. Bitty saw *opposite* again, underlined twice and then:

copper? brass?
coils and water
Find better product name!!

Across the bottom of the page, in printed letters, with a signature beneath them, were the words *Property of Virgil P. Smith, inventor.*

The Whatchamacallit! If they could convince the mine owners to use it, maybe then the canaries could get out! Other mines had replaced canaries with "new-fangled machinery," as Uncle Aubrey called it. And this would be even newer. Better! There was the price to worry about—the company made the miners pay for most of their equipment themselves, from their coal picks and shovels right up to their headlamps—but this seemed different somehow.

Bitty turned his head sideways to study the sketch from another angle. It was then that he saw, stalking slowly into the room, as if he were the one who had booked it, another of Miss Alma's cats. The movement of Bitty's head caught the cat's attention. The creature stalked toward him—and the table.

Bitty flew toward the bed, knowing the cat would follow. The cat did, and lunged. Bitty dodged the attack with no trouble. The gray cat pounced again as Bitty flew to the top of the suitcase, wishing he had the seagulls' ability to hover. The cat followed. Bitty zipped across the room again. It was almost fun. He could see why Eck liked his job. With the cat's attention turned toward Bitty, Eck made his way quietly toward the mouse hole. But the cat saw him and lunged again. Bitty heard a squeak that sounded like pain in any language.

"*FEE-YO. FEE-YO!*" Bitty flew back and forth, trying to regain the cat's attention. "*FEE-YO!*" With a low growl, the cat switched directions again. He jumped and caught air.

"Missed me!" Bitty shouted, but it was more relief than bragging. The cat jumped again. He missed the bird, but he hit the rickety table that held the invention. Everything moved in slow motion. The table fell toward the floor and the invention began to slide. Bitty swooped in, as if he had enough strength to stop it. Then everything rushed into real time again. The gas detector crashed to the floor, the copper separating along the seam where it had been fused, the glass shattering into slivers. The cat froze, but only for a moment. Bitty turned to follow Eck into the hole, but the base of the Whatchamacallit had landed on his tail feathers. Bitty struggled forward with a jerk. He felt a tug and then a pop as the movement plucked one long yellow feather from his rear end. It lay beneath what was left of the Whatchamacallit like a flower petal in a junkyard. Bitty kept plunging forward, finally making it to the safety of the hole, where he found Eck nursing a J-shaped wound that started on one side of his tail and ended on the other. He had a deep scratch near his eye as well.

"Sorry," Eck and Bitty said at the same time.

"Are you okay?" they both asked. Bitty would have called "Jinx" and punched Eck in the arm, but his friend had been through enough.

"It was my fault," Bitty said. "I made us come in here. Now I've ruined everything."

"I should have been paying more attention," Eck said. "These creatures are in my charge, after all."

The door of the room was pushed wider open, and a man—Virgil P. Smith, it had to be—entered. He was tall and thin and rumpled-looking, as if he had just gotten out of bed. He cursed the cat, went straight to the table and righted it. As he bent to gather up the metal casing and its tangled innards, he paused. "What in the name of—?" He picked up Bitty's feather. Then he looked at the cat again. "What did you do, puss? Open up." But the cat's mouth stayed closed and he walked slowly from the room, his business there complete.

Thoughtfully, the man twirled the tail feather between his thumb and first finger. He set it carefully on the nightstand, then bent to the floor again and tried to sweep up some of the broken glass with his hand. "Alma," he shouted. "I'll be needing a broom."

He snatched his hand back and squeezed it shut, but not before Bitty saw a drop of red.

"And a bandage, Alma," Virgil Smith added. He had a face that was probably kind most of the time. But now it wore a look that was worse than anger; it was a look of defeat.

Bitty's remaining tailfeathers drooped. He had come with a mission: to find help. He'd messed things up instead. "I should go," he told Eck. "You'll let me know if he fixes it?"

"Of course," the mouse said, rubbing his rump. "I'll send you a message."

"A message?"

"Naturally." Eck led the way back to the warm room, where Bonnie fussed over his injuries. "We have a very sophisticated system."

"If you can get a message to me across town, could I get a message to someone out of town? To Coalbank Hollow?"

"Of course," Eck said. "Haven't you ever received a message before?"

"Never."

"There. All fixed," Bonnie said. Then, "Well, of course he's never gotten a message. Who would he know on the outside?" She looked at Bitty. "Homesick so soon?" She said it seriously, not teasing—knowing, perhaps, that Bitty felt as fragile as the invention he'd just destroyed.

"Not for the place," he said. "It's just that Aunt Lou's a worrier and Alice—"

"A girl. Say no more!" Eck said. "I'll tell you everything I know about sending messages. Though it's your kind that's in charge of the telephone company. Not mine."

"My kind? You mean canaries?"

"Well, no, not canaries per se, " Eck said. "Birdkind. You're the ones who fly all over creation, so it's easy for you to get messages back and forth. I'm told there's quite an advanced relay system. And territories. And zones."

"Zones?"

"It's not as confusing as it sounds," Eck said.

"It's not as confusing as he's making it," Bonnie joined in, giving Eck a gentle jab in the ribs.

Eck winced but grinned. "Look, it's simple, really. All you have to do is talk to a bird on a wire."

"A telephone wire?"

"Exactly. Mourning doves, they're up there a lot. And purple martins and grackles."

At the word *grackle,* Bitty cringed.

"Forget I said grackle," Eck told him. "Kingfishers. Barn swallows. Any bird on a wire is on duty, see? You give them your message and they'll send it out. It should get to Coalbank Hollow in a day or two, give or take a week."

Bitty thanked his friend, took a crumble of the inn's famous corn bread for the walk through the tunnel, and said his final good-bye.

"Be careful of hawks," Eck said. "They usually attack when you're alone, you know."

"I've heard that," Bitty said.

"You'll be safe with the pigeons. And try not to worry. I'm sure the inventor will fix the Whosawhatsit. If it ever worked in the first place."

Trying not to think of the solo flight between the mouse hole and the train station, Bitty made his way up the dark tunnel. If a vein of hard coal had replaced the mouse-chewed wood and earth (and if it had been a little larger) it would have felt exactly like Coalbank Hollow.

Bitty emerged from the mouse hole and found the world as dark as the tunnel. Of course—it was evening now. He had lost all track of time inside the walls of the inn. The legislators had probably gone home for the day. It must be way past dinnertime, and he'd promised to meet Clarence. He thought about sending his message home—he could see the black silhouettes of two birds on a telephone wire—but decided the best move was to return to the station. Fast.

Bitty flew through the East End and crossed the river, hovering over the bridge again, for safety. He didn't look down until he'd made it to the roof of the train station.

Below him, humans called out to each other once again. But up here, all was quiet, save for the gentle cooing of the pigeons. Clarence was already asleep. Bitty scouted out a spot in the gutter a few feet away and tested it for signs of moisture. The tin was cold to the touch, but he found a few sticks for his bed frame. On the ground behind the station he found a piece of cotton and a swath of cloth, and with those materials he built his first nest. If the folks at home could see this! It was his one success. He didn't want them to know about his failures.

Bitty looked up at the night sky and drew in a breath. Back home, he could see only a few stars, shining like cut glass on the small strip of sky that was visible from Jamie's bedroom window. But here? Bitty couldn't even count them all. There must be hundreds. Thousands! He felt as if he could fly up and touch them. He felt as if he could catch them like the summer fireflies that sometimes glowed from a Mason jar on Jamie's nightstand. He wondered if he could see every star in the sky. And he wondered how many of those stars were shining over Coalbank Hollow.

Chapter 13

Bitty slept the restless sleep that comes from being in a strange place. He dreamed he was in the coal mine, only this time, he wasn't in a cage. He was free to zip through the tunnels, a blurry speck of yellow in a black world. As he flew, the miners slapped at him the way he'd seen Jamie slap mosquitoes.

"I'm free," Bitty told them, though of course none of them spoke Bird. "Mountainy Liberty. I mean, monetary library. *Montani Semper Liberi.* Leave me alone. I'm free."

The tips of the Gap-Toothed Man's pudgy fingers flicked Bitty on the head.

Thwack.

There they were again.

Bitty opened his eyes and saw not the miner's fingers, but Clarence peering down at him.

Peck. Clarence poked Bitty in the head for the third time. "Come on, sleepyhead, get up. My mom says if I work this morning, I can show you around this afternoon. You can help."

"What time is it?" Despite years of waking up before the sun, this morning, the sun had beaten him.

"It's six-thirty, so we've got to move. Old humans wake up earlier than the rest."

Sure enough, Mrs. Gillespie was already sitting on a bench.

Bitty took a bath in the creek to make sure he looked and smelled his best for the legislators—and Clarence's clients. Then he joined the pigeon near Mrs. Gillespie. Her hands were curled like claws, but she dropped a piece of a sticky bun on the ground by her feet.

"Come on," Clarence called. "She doesn't bite."

Bitty looked again at the curled hands, then tried a taste of sticky bun.

"Why, hello, pretty," Mrs. Gillespie said.

"She means you," Clarence told him. "She calls me 'precious.'"

"*Girls* are pretty," Bitty said.

"She's a little gushy. But you get used to it."

For a full hour they sat with Mrs. Gillespie, who went back and forth between cooing at them in baby talk that was more sugary than the sticky buns and railing about President Hoover.

Their next client blew his nose like an elephant. Instead of calling Bitty "pretty," he went with "*Serinus canaria domestica*," which made him sound as formal as Eck. He didn't offer them any bread, though, so they moved on to Hobo Pete.

"I need to get to the courthouse," Bitty said.

"But Pete's the best. You've gotta meet him."

They approached a bench and found a tall, scruffy man with newspaper draped over his legs like a blanket. Bitty tried to read some of the stories, but the news was old and the words were too wrinkled to read.

"I'm surprised you found enough stuff for your nest with him around," Clarence said. "Hobo Pete is the best scrap finder in the city." The man's enormous shoes were laced with brown twine. He had patched the soles with newspaper and masking tape. The birds waited as he pulled a crumpled paper bag from his belongings. He reached inside and came up with some bread crumbs for them. Then he leaned back and shook the rest of the bag's contents into his mouth.

When his throat was clear, he began to speak: "Did I ever tell you about the train I caught when I was coming through Virginia? The stationmaster, he had only one eye, see, but it was a sharp eye and he kept it on the boxcars. They were full of cabbage. Don't know a soul who likes cabbage...."

Two more clients. Two more hours of listening. Then they could do as they pleased.

"Farmers' market next?" asked Clarence.

"Courthouse," Bitty repeated. "I need to find a lawmaker."

"But I introduced you to one already," Clarence said.

"Who? Hobo Pete?"

"No, the other guy, the one who called you the fancy name."

"The nose honker?" For some reason, it had never occurred to Bitty that a politician could be short and bald. He looked back toward the bench, but the man had gone.

"What did you aim to do once you found him, anyway?" Clarence asked.

"Well, I was hoping to...," Bitty said. "And then I was gonna..." What *was* he going to do? Stick a lump of coal in the lawmaker's sock? Play dead on the man's desk and see if he got the point? Challenge him to a game of charades?

Bitty sighed. He had a mission. What he didn't have, apparently, was a decent plan. It was time to make one.

"Look, I don't know too much about how it all works," Clarence said. "But I know they have committees that look into things. Maybe there's a committee that looks into animal safety."

"Maybe," Bitty said. It sounded as good as anything he'd come up with.

"So," Clarence said. "Should I help you find the courthouse?"

"Yup," Bitty said. He looked up and saw a bird on a wire. "But first I need to call—" He almost said "Alice" but at the last second changed it to "home."

"Look for the wires without the grackles," Clarence advised.

Bitty had learned that much already. The nearest bird was a sparrow. She was a dusty brown color, but she had a stripe near her eye that made it look as if she was built for speed. "How about her?" he said.

"That's Miss Mona," Clarence said. "She's the best. Do you want me to introduce you?"

"I can handle it." Bitty was eager to prove he could do something on his own. "I'll meet you in a minute."

"I'll be in the market by the sweet potato pies," Clarence said.

"Got it." Bitty flew to the wire and landed.

"Operator," Miss Mona said. "May I help you?"

"I'd like to send a message to Coalbank Hollow, West Virginia, please."

"Where in Coalbank Hollow do you wish to send it?" The bird spoke in a short, clipped voice. Her head moved with each syllable.

"I'd like to send it to Two One Two Slusser Road," Bitty told her. "To the Big House in Jamie's bedroom. Address it: 'To all canaries present.'"

"And who is the message from, sir?"

"From me. I mean, from Bitty."

"Proceed."

"If you could just tell them I'm in Charleston, please, and that I'm living at the train station. With some pigeons, who aren't really lazy at all, Uncle Aubrey was wrong about that. And tell them I'm doing just fine. And that I miss them. I've met a mouse. And they should come visit soon, though they should be careful of the—"

"Let me repeat your message to make sure I've got it right: Bitty safe at Char depot with pigs. Stop. Visit. Stop. Will that be all?"

"Pigs?"

"It's short for pigeons," Miss Mona said. "Everyone knows that."

"Well, what about the pigeons not being lazy? What about my missing them at home?"

"We have to eliminate unnecessary words so the messages are easier to remember," Miss Mona said. "Your friends probably know you miss them. And *everybody* knows pigeons aren't lazy. They're just overweight. Speaking of overweight," the sparrow said as the wire beneath them sagged. Bitty turned to see a puffy-cheeked squirrel hurrying toward them. Soon the squirrel and the sparrow were engaged in a rapid conversation. Bitty couldn't understand a single word. At first he thought it was because of the nuts in the squirrel's mouth, which had the same effect as the plugs of tobacco that sometimes garbled the speech of the miners. Then he realized it was a whole different language. The squirrel twitched his ears, uttered what sounded like a bark and ran off again. The telephone wire bounced in his wake.

"You speak Squirrel?" Bitty asked.

"I speak a dozen languages," Miss Mona said. "Bird, of course, and Squirrel. I also speak Cat, Dog, Mouse, Mole, Chipmunk, Snake, Lizard, Bear and Rabbit. Oh, and Armadillo, though I don't get much chance to use it here." She looked at Bitty hopefully. "Do *you* speak Armadillo?"

"Just Bird," Bitty said. "And Human. That is, I understand Human if somebody else speaks it." He had tried a few times to speak it himself, to Jamie, but without lips nothing sounded right.

"Only Bird?" Miss Mona said. "How do you manage?"

"I haven't really needed to know any other languages up until now," he said. "I was living in a cage."

"I understand. Perfectly," Miss Mona said. "But you're in the world now; effective communication is important. If you ever want to learn another language, I do offer classes, you know. Miss Mona's Language School for the Natural World."

"I don't suppose you could teach me enough Human to speak before the West Virginia legislature?" Bitty explained about his mission.

Miss Mona sighed. "Humans are so difficult. But other animals? Easy peasy."

Bitty thought about that. If he was trying to get the word out about the miners' plight, why not spread it as many places as possible?

"We meet beneath that snowball bush every day at three," Miss Mona said.

"I'll be there," Bitty said. He thanked the operator and crossed the river, hovering over the bridge once again. He found Clarence near the pies on the other side. They were able to share a few flakes after Clarence hollered at the sparrows (who weren't nearly as polite as Miss Mona): "Hey! How about saving some for the new guy?"

Then they flew to Court Street.

The stone courthouse loomed before them, the color of sand. It wasn't as impressive as the capitol. Still, people passed laws inside. Could they outlaw the use of canaries as guinea pigs? Force West Virginia to improve the conditions down in the mines?

A cardinal ("capital birds," Bitty remembered) stood sentry by the arched doorway, his red plumage contrasting with the stone. Bitty and Clarence flew straight to him. Bitty cleared his throat, but the cardinal spoke first.

"Hear ye, hear ye. Welcome to the temporary quarters of the West Virginia General Assembly. State your name."

"Bitty."

"State your business."

"I want to find the legislators who are involved with animal safety. And coal mining."

"State your purpose."

"I need to talk to them," Bitty said. "About the conditions in the mines and the fact that every day, men are putting their own lives and the lives of innocent birds at risk."

The cardinal leaned forward, his crested head nearly touching Bitty's own, and his air of formality was replaced with an air of incredulity. "I'm sorry, son, did you say you wanted to *talk* to them?"

Bitty swallowed. "Or something," he said.

The bird stood straight again and breathed deeply. "If I were you," he said, "I'd file a report. Of course, you could also stage a protest—I love a good protest. But I'm afraid they're not always effective."

"But a report—?"

"In all honesty, they're not always effective, either. But they don't require a permit. Or a crowd."

A report, then! There would be no need for lips. Bitty could present his case with written documents about the canaries' plight. He'd bring the lawmakers newspaper articles about the conditions in the mine and the dangers to workers and canaries. He could talk about the size of their cages, the dampness and the cold. Except that no one seemed to be writing newspaper articles about canaries. He'd have to find a way to write his own. He couldn't pick up a pencil or scratch his report out on a slate; but he could use words that were already written for him. He'd find clippings. He'd turn them into a report. He'd—

"Of course you'd still need to present it," the cardinal said, as if he could read Bitty's mind. "To the appropriate committee."

"Which would be...?" Bitty and Clarence waited for the answer.

"The Committee on Mines and Mining, of course," the cardinal responded.

"And they meet...?" Clarence prodded.

"In ten days."

"Ten days?" Bitty wanted to talk to someone sooner than that! The clock was ticking. On the other hand, it would take time to write his report.

The cardinal indicated a calendar that was posted on the glass door.

Committee on Mines and Mining: Wednesday, 9 a.m.

"That's it," Bitty said. "That's where I need to be."

"Excellent, young squire." The bird winked at him. "The name's Cato, should you need any help in the future. I'm happy to be of service."

Now that his plan was taking shape, Bitty's days were open as wide as the blossom of a mayapple. He filled them up. In the early mornings, he went with Clarence to visit the elderly and ate enough to last most of the day. The politician had been back to his bench only once, and he'd clucked at them softly and made some notes in a book. Bitty hoped the man would be on the Committee on Mines and Mining. He was a familiar face, at least, and while he still hadn't fed the birds, it was clear that he liked them.

Bitty spent the late mornings searching for scraps of paper so he could work on his mining manifesto. Clarence was right—Hobo Pete grabbed every scrap that wasn't nailed down. But Bitty didn't hold it against him. The best mornings began when the man rubbed his beard, shook some crumbs out of his bag and said, "Now, where was I? Oh yes, the winter of twenty-nine…"

Clarence liked the hobo so much that he wrote a poem about him, and Bitty memorized it:

Hobo Pete,
He had no meat,
So he dined on day-old bread.
He took a little smidgen
And gave it to a pigeon,
And he went to bed well fed.

Had it been Bitty's poem, he would have added something about the hobo's feet, which also rhymed with *Pete.* But he was no expert; the only other poem he even knew was "Gone, Birdie, Gone." He liked the sentiments of Clarence's poem much better, even if the hobo was far from well fed.

Afternoons were spent exploring and studying the work habits of other birds, who were returning to the city as spring came on full-force. When Clarence suggested the dump one afternoon, Bitty agreed, though he was worried. It was because of Cipher that he'd ended up at the dump in the first place, and it would be a long flight, through open air. He hadn't seen the hawk all week, but that didn't mean she wasn't out there someplace, watching.

Bitty tried to be pragmatic. Hawks had big noses, so they probably wouldn't spend much time near the dump. Plus, Bitty would be with Clarence. Dolly and Eck said hawks usually attacked when their victims were alone.

There were more reasons to go to the dump. There were bound to be newspapers, for one thing. He wanted to see if Phil and Gladys had spotted anything special in the inn's trash. And he wanted to prove that he wasn't hoity-toity.

They set off, scanning the sky as they flew. Bitty's chest felt like a fiddle string wound too tightly, but there was no sign of the hawk. Bitty's flying was getting stronger. He already had more stamina than Clarence, who was a city bird and not used to flying very far. Plus, Clarence had to hold up all that extra weight.

They landed side by side on a steel girder overlooking a mountain of garbage. The white birds were still there, floating on air.

"Phil, look!" Gladys yelled. "It's Bitty. He came back."

"Hey, Kid Canary," said Phil. "You lost again? If we'd known you were coming we'd have saved you some corn bread."

"That's all right," Bitty said. "I was hoping for something else. Something inedible." He asked his question about the inn's garbage.

The birds led him to the spot, but Bitty found nothing beyond the usual vegetable peelings and a kitchen fan that was broken beyond all repair. Did that mean that Mr. Smith was working again? Or had he abandoned his project completely?

"How's it going, kid?" Phil asked. "Have you saved your friends yet?"

"Not yet."

"If it helps, we told everyone here all about it. If it were up to us, we'd make some changes in those mines. We're behind you, just so you know."

"Thanks."

Bitty and Clarence scouted around for bits of newspaper and other things with writing on them. Much of what they found was soggy, but they came across a few pieces that were respectable enough. They stayed at the dump until Gladys offered to share some of her minced clams. Then they flew home.

At three, as promised, Bitty attended Miss Mona's language school and became part of a class that featured two cardinals, including Cato, the bird he'd met at the courthouse, one duck ("They're company birds, too," Clarence explained, "only they specialize in children and we deal in geriatrics") and the puffy-cheeked squirrel who had made the wire sag when Bitty had sent that first message through Miss Mona—a message that had, as of yet, received no reply.

On the first day, they learned to exchange niceties with a Screaming Hairy Armadillo. "Because if you ever do meet a Screaming Hairy Armadillo, it is most important to be nice," Miss Mona added. "Now, repeat after me." She grunted twice, like a hungry pig.

"*Grrruunt.*" Bitty's classmates duplicated the sound perfectly.

"Excellent," Miss Mona said. "You have just told an armadillo to have a nice day. Bitty?"

"*Rirk,*" Bitty said. "Excuse me. Maybe if I just...*Rirk.*"

"Nice try, dear, but I fear the armadillo would take offense. Keep practicing and the sounds will become easier to make. The world, students, is filled with sounds, which we can all mimic if we just pay attention. Now repeat after me: *Meowow prrrrrrrt.*"

"*Ow krrrrrt,*" Bitty began, almost learning to say "Where is the bathroom?" in Cat, which seemed completely unnecessary, as birds did not require bathrooms—nor did squirrels, as far as he knew. There were other, more important words Bitty wanted to learn. *Union,* for instance, and *help.* Also: *prisoners, mines, greedy, coal operators, dangerous conditions* and *completely unfair.* Effective communication *was* important. Miss Mona had said so herself. And part of his mission was to tell everyone he could about the mines and the miners, human and bird alike.

The second class was more intense. By the third, Bitty had learned enough conversational Squirrel to be able to relay, in simple sentences: "The mine is dangerous. There is more we can do."

"Could you teach me...How do you say *friend* in Mouse?" he asked Miss Mona at the end of his fifth class. He owed Eck another visit, and he wanted to impress him.

"The word is *eeni,*" Miss Mona said.

"*Eeni,*" Bitty repeated slowly.

"Perfect. You got that one exactly right."

On his way back to the passenger station, Bitty found a scrap of paper. This one had no words, but it was exactly what he needed.

With the aid of some pinesap, he arranged the words from the bits of newspaper he'd collected so far and stuck them on. It was more of a letter than an article or report. It wasn't quite a manifesto. But he thought it got his point across.

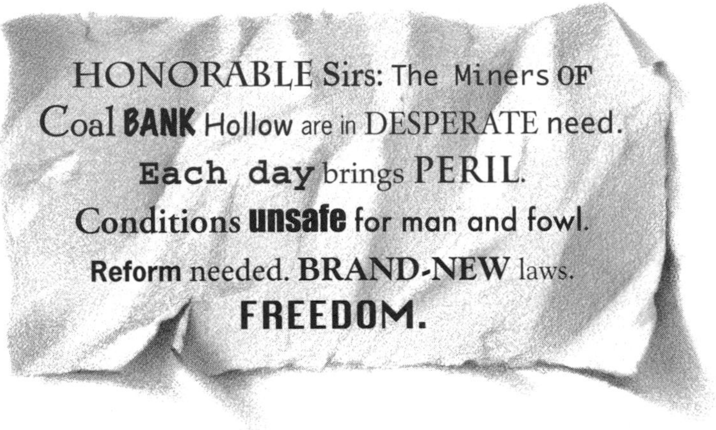

HONORABLE Sirs: The Miners OF
Coal BANK Hollow are in DESPERATE need.
Each day brings PERIL.
Conditions unsafe for man and fowl.
Reform needed. BRAND-NEW laws.
FREEDOM.

It wasn't perfect. Bitty knew Uncle Aubrey would take offense at the use of the word *fowl*, but he hadn't been able to find *canaries* in the papers he'd snagged, or even the more generic *birds*. With a little more tweaking, he would be able to make his point.

The next day, Clarence took him to see Walter, another sparrow, whose ear was pressed against the telephone wire.

"An operator?" Bitty guessed.

"Nope," Clarence said.

"What's he doing, then?"

"Walter's a she."

"Well, what's *she* doing?" Bitty said.

"Getting the news."

Walter lifted her head from the wire and spoke: "Earthquake in Nicaragua. Here in the States, the economy continues its downward spiral. In Harlan, Kentucky, the coal strike continues and out-of-work miners are near starvation, witnesses report. And in local news, there was a fight outside the theater, which was showing *Chickens Come*

Home. The movie was *not* the reason for the brawl. In weather, thunderstorms are expected and rain will be heavy at times. In fact..."
She stuck out her wing just as a giant drop fell from the sky. "Time to take cover." She weighed so little that the wire didn't even swing when she flew away.

"We'd better get back to the station," Clarence said. The rumbling sky agreed.

In Coalbank Hollow, Bitty had seen gray clouds snagged on the mountaintop. He'd felt the drops as he'd been transported from the mine to Jamie's room. But he'd never been in a storm like this. Mr. Campbell would have said it was "raining pitchforks." By the time they got back to the station, Bitty's feathers were soaked.

"What do you do when it rains?" he yelled to Clarence over the rat-a-tat-tat of the drops. Thunder boomed.

"It depends," Clarence yelled back. "Sometimes we hit the trees. Mostly we just stand on the balcony—there's some cover there."

Bitty thought about the grackles in the trees and opted for a spot near his friends. The driving rain angled in on him. Water spit at his feet. The pigeons, who were used to storms, huddled together against the brick. Bitty stood beside them, shivering, until Clarence's mother reached out a wing and pulled him in.

Chapter 14

The rain fell in silver sheets. There were no humans on the park benches, so Bitty and the pigeons stayed on the balcony, hugging the building for warmth and finding none. Every now and then, a pigeon would leave to scout for food left by the passengers. But with the rain, the passengers hurried from one spot to the next, clutching their umbrellas; they didn't spend much time eating, and when the pigeons did find food, it was so soggy it disintegrated on contact.

Finally, after a day and a half, the gray skies parted. The rain stopped. White clouds hovered low, as if the mountains were blowing smoke rings. Then they, too, lifted and the sun appeared, drying the station and the ground and the gutter. A little shaky from lack of food, Bitty flew up to inspect the remains of his nest. He found one twig lodged near the top of the drainpipe; that was all. But worse than the destruction of his new home: his letter to the mining committee had disappeared completely. He checked the ground beneath the drainpipe. It wasn't there, either. He couldn't find one word that he'd collected and pasted. And the Committee on Mines and Mining was scheduled to meet the day after tomorrow.

"You can write a new note," Clarence said. "But you'd better make it quick."

"I know." Bitty's voice warbled strangely. His chest hurt. He shivered, despite the sun, which might as well have been made of ice instead of fire.

"*Achooo.*"

"*Gesundheit,*" Clarence said. "Hey. Maybe you're catching a cold."

"*Achoooo.*"

"Rain'll do it to you," Clarence said. "I'll get my mom. She always takes care of me when I'm sick."

Bitty didn't tell Clarence how dangerous a cold could be for a canary. His throat felt as if he'd swallowed a porcupine.

"Oh, poor dear," Clarence's mother said when she saw Bitty, whose eyes were watery and who, now that he knew he was sick, was coughing nonstop. "We need to get you warm, that's all. You'll be fine in a jiffy."

"Wh-wh-where's it warm?" Bitty asked.

"I know a spot," Clarence's mother said. "Inside."

"Inside?" Clarence said. "But the last time—"

"Inside," his mother said. "If only a few of us go, we won't be caught."

The birds moved close to the heavy doors that led from the balcony to the second-floor waiting room. The next time someone stepped out for a breath of air, Bitty followed the pigeons into the station and headed straight for the ceiling.

"This way, this way," Clarence's mother said. She led him to a high beam bathed in sunshine, which was streaming through the arched windows. There was no wind. Bitty could now see not just the waiting room, which covered only part of the second floor, but all the way down to the great room below.

"My letter—" Bitty was coughing too much to finish his sentence.

"He's got a fever," Clarence's mother told her son. "Find something we can use as a blanket. A piece of fabric or . . . that. That would be a perfect nest."

Bitty followed her gaze to the room below, where a woman sat perched on her suitcase, wearing a red wool hat.

"Won't she miss it?" Clarence said.

"That hat's too warm for this time of year," Clarence's mother said. "We'd be doing her a favor."

"If I take it, they'll spot us." Clarence looked at Bitty, who shivered back at him. "Okay. I'll try."

The pigeon did a perfect dive toward the lady's head. He snagged the hat with his brick-red feet and started to carry it skyward.

"*Thief!*" the woman shrieked. "A lady never goes anywhere without a hat!"

The humans looked around, perhaps for a pickpocket. When they spotted Clarence, they pointed and laughed. He looked like a flying strawberry. Bitty laughed, too, but his laugh turned into another cough as Clarence landed, breathless, on the beam beside him.

"Good work," said Clarence's mother. She laid out the hat like a sleeping bag and Bitty climbed inside. Warm at last, he slept. When he awoke a few hours later, he was tired and dizzy and hot. Clarence's mother dropped some water from her beak and Bitty opened his mouth to catch it. He felt like a baby. He swallowed and slept again.

Sometimes he opened his eyes and saw Clarence beside him. Sometimes it was Clarence's mother or Miss Mona or Dolly, the chimney swift. Once he saw Aunt Lou and called to her, wondering how she had found him, but she disappeared without answering. The next time he awoke, it was his mother and father he saw, dancing. Bitty danced with them, his wings touching theirs.

"Dance with us," he told Clarence when he opened his eyes and found his friend beside him. But Clarence just gave him a worried look and hurried away. When Bitty closed his eyes again, his parents had gone, too. *Everybody keeps leaving,* he thought, and then he remembered: he was the one who'd left. He slept again and dreamed of home.

He woke up hungry. Clarence was sitting with him and whooped when Bitty asked for food.

"You got it," he said, and disappeared into the station. He came back with a piece of cinnamon bun. "I was saving it," he said, "for when you were well."

"How long have I been out?" Bitty asked.

"Five days."

"That's almost a week!" Bitty said. "I missed the committee meeting. I've got to—"

"First things first, dear," said Clarence's mother, who had come to check on her patient. She put a gray wing against his forehead. "Fever's dropped. But I want you in bed for the rest of the day. Tomorrow you can get back to work."

He'd lost six days already. Now it had been fifty-two days since Boggs had died, which left fifty-one days until the record. But it was called the record for a reason. Sometimes the accidents didn't wait. Bitty couldn't wait, either.

"I've got to go," he said.

"You've already missed the meeting," Clarence reminded him. "One more day won't hurt."

"You could have gone to the meeting for me." Bitty sounded meaner than he meant to. "You could have written a new letter."

"Aw, I'm not as good with words as you are."

"You wrote that poem."

"But *you're* the canary," Clarence said. "How would it look, getting a report on mining conditions from a pigeon? I don't know a coal mine from a drinking well. Listen, we can still go find your politicians. We can still get the letter to the right place."

"But I—"

"You can't help anybody if you don't get completely well. You just need a plan B."

Bitty sighed. At the rate he was going, he needed a plan for every letter of the alphabet. He nibbled on a piece of his cinnamon bun, which made him feel a little better. He finally remembered to thank Clarence, which he should have done first thing.

"I'm sorry," Bitty said. "I'm mad at myself, mostly." He wished again that he had been able to talk Miss Mona into including "pigeons aren't lazy" in his message to the Big House. Which reminded him:

"I didn't get a message from Coalbank Hollow, did I?"

Clarence wobbled his head "no."

Bitty shivered, as if he still had a fever. Maybe his message had never reached the hollow. It was better to think about that than to think about all the reasons his friends might not have sent a message back. He brushed the thoughts away. "Thanks," he told Clarence. "For everything."

Clarence shrugged. "Well, after all, I'm a company bird."

The next morning Bitty took a short test flight around the station. Then, when a man stepped onto the balcony to light up a cigarette, Bitty shot outside. The fresh air felt wonderful. It had grown warmer during the week, and the tulip magnolias were in full bloom now, their pale pink blossoms enveloping brown branches in soft pink clouds. Bitty flew behind the station to what he had started referring to as Grackle Creek and tasted the sweet water as it rushed down the mountain to meet him. V and the Boys screamed at him from the trees above, but they did not swarm or send torpedoes, and Bitty stood firmly on his rock. He didn't leave until he'd drunk his fill.

He wanted to go see Miss Mona, and to visit the temporary capitol to see when the next mining meeting had been scheduled. But he figured the least he could do was to join Clarence on his morning rounds first. He owed him. Besides, he could keep an eye out for more newspaper.

Mrs. Gillespie greeted him with a shower of bread. "Hello, pretty. I wondered what happened to my pretty."

"I'm back," Bitty chirped without coughing.

Hobo Pete had given up his bench, but they found him lounging under a maple, his beard looking scruffier than ever.

"Sorry, friends," the hobo said. "I got nothing today. No crumbs. No stories. Might be time to strike out and find some new ones." Bitty stood near Pete's left knee, but the man remained silent. It was time to move on.

When their shift was over, they flew back to Court Street and landed on the steps of the courthouse. The calendar that was posted on the door didn't list any more meetings for the Committee on Mines and Mining; it didn't list anything at all. Bitty spotted Cato, with his red fathers and black goatee.

"Hello, young squire. How are you feeling?" the cardinal asked.

"Lousy," Bitty said. "I missed the mining meeting and I need to find someone to help me. Is there anyone inside? Someone on the committee?"

"The only person in there right now is the judge, son," Cato said. "Session's over."

"What?" Bitty must have heard wrong.

"The legislative session has ended," Cato repeated. "I'm afraid everyone's gone home."

"Home? For how long?" Why, why, why had he gotten sick?

"Let's see. Unless they call an extra session, no one will be back until... January."

"January?" Bitty looked at Clarence, who wobbled his head sympathetically. "I can't wait. I've waited too long already."

"Well, now, hold on, let's see," Cato said, backtracking. "When I said everyone's gone home, I didn't mean they'd all gone *directly* home. You might find a few still about the city, tying up some loose ends, as it were. Maybe you can make a direct appeal."

"Is there anyone here from Coalbank Hollow?" Clarence asked.

Of course! Bitty should have thought of that.

"The Honorable Delegate Finch lives somewhere near Coalbank. He's a real bird lover, too," the cardinal said. He looked at Clarence. "You'd know where to find him better than I would."

"I never heard him mention Coalbank Hollow," Clarence said.

"Wait," Bitty said. "You know him?"

"Yeah, and so do you," Clarence said. "He's the nose honker. But he wasn't in the park this morning. I only saw him once while you were sick."

"You might try the new capitol," Cato suggested. "Some of them like to go there to watch the progress. And Bitty: if I see anyone come by here, I'll get a message to you. You've got a worthy cause. I want to help."

Plan C. Bitty and Clarence set off again, weaving quickly through the streets of the East End, until they came upon the construction site. The main building stood, already majestic, alongside the river, just across from the university. The dome was farther along than it had been when Bitty first arrived in Charleston, but he still didn't trust it.

Some distance away, resting on an outcropping of rock, he saw two men, their backs to the river. Each man had a pair of binoculars dangling around his neck.

Bitty heard a familiar honk and saw one of them blowing into a handkerchief. He looked somehow taller than he had on the bench, and less bald. Mr. Campbell always said the politicians he knew were "crooked as a dog's hind leg." And he thought the capitol building was a gold-plated luxury, given the times. Still, Bitty couldn't help being impressed.

The birds landed, hidden by the tall grass. The hammering on the capitol was far enough away that they could overhear the two men.

"By the time we come back, she'll be done," said Mr. Finch.

"Yep," said his friend.

"For better or for worse," said Mr. Finch.

"Yep."

"You know, I saw the old one burn?"

"You been here that long?"

"Fire was right after New Year's," said Mr. Finch. "They'd stored the guns they'd confiscated from the mine wars up on the top floor, and when it went up? *Whoo-ee*, let me tell you. It was like fireworks. Of course, no one was celebrating. We were running, is what we were doing."

"Those miners went crazy, didn't they?" said the man who was not Mr. Finch.

Crazy? Bitty thought. Uncle Aubrey had always described it as the miners' finest moment—standing up to the coal operators and their hired hands, to corrupt politicians and the government. Of course, they'd lost in the end, but they'd been on the front page of the *Charleston Gazette* and newspapers everywhere else, too. People knew about them. Then they forgot.

"They were trying to get someone to listen," said Mr. Finch. "We plugged our ears. You know, my brother used to be a doctor in a coal camp—his first job out of medical school. The things he saw! Men with their legs crushed. And no money waiting for them when they couldn't work anymore. The miners, though, they took care of their own. Tried to, anyway."

"*Mmm-mmm.*" The man shook his head. "When are you headed back?"

"Thursday. You?"

"Same."

"You want to meet up Wednesday morning, then?" the politician asked.

"Yep."

"Round eight?"

The man stood and began walking away. Mr. Finch stayed on the rock another moment, gazing at the building. Then he turned his binoculars toward the river.

"A grebe! A horned grebe!" he said, pulling a notebook from his breast pocket. Boldly, Bitty lit on the rock beside him.

Delegate Finch looked down. "Well, well. It's my canary friend, is it?"

Bitty stared at him, willing the man to read his mind. The man stared back, waiting.

"Is this supposed to be part of the plan?" Clarence called from the grass.

"*Shhh.* Yes."

Slowly, the man put his hands to his lips. "Howdy!" he said distinctly in Bird. He said it again. "Howdy!"

"He speaks Bird!" Bitty yelled. At last! A breakthrough! He turned back to Mr. Finch. "It's an honor to meet you, sir. I'm Bitty, a canary from Coalbank Hollow, and we need your help."

"Howdy!" said Mr. Finch.

"Um, *howdy*," Bitty repeated. "As I was saying, my friends and I work at the Number Seven mine and we risk our lives every day. But there's other equipment that can detect gas *almost* as well as we can. And, sir? The mine has bad ventilation. The company doesn't treat the miners the way people should be treated, and you're a politician. You could make things better. You could pass another law—"

"Howdy!" said Mr. Finch. "Howdy! Howdy! Howdy!"

Bitty stopped talking and looked at Clarence. This wasn't a proper response at all. Was this what Uncle Aubrey meant when he talked about "crazy politicians"? Mr. Finch took his hands away from his lips, and Bitty saw a glimmer of metal. A bird whistle.

"I should have known," Bitty said, kicking the rock. "He doesn't speak Bird at all."

"We'll just have to find another way," Clarence said, waddling out of his hiding place.

Plan D.

"Yeah," Bitty said. "By Wednesday morning. Come on. Let's go see Miss Mona and Walter. I need to find out what else I slept through."

As they flew off, they heard Mr. Finch holler "Howdy!" one more time. When they looked back, he was watching them with his binoculars. Then his attention shifted back to the grebe.

Chapter 15

Aunt Lou always said no news was good news. Bitty didn't believe that. Sometimes, no news meant the worst. He checked in with Miss Mona first, and Bitty greeted her in Bird, Cat and Squirrel. Miss Mona returned the greeting but had no message from the Big House.

"I wish I did," she said, shifting her feet to keep her balance on the wire, which was sagging a bit under Clarence's weight. "But I do have a message from your mouse friend."

"Eck? What did he say?"

" 'Inventor back at work,' " she said. " 'Visit.' "

"Well, at least that's good news," Bitty said.

"And that's not all. Your classmates are telling your story to everyone they know. They're behind you, Bitty. We all are."

That just left the humans to win over.

Bitty and Clarence went in search of Walter next. They found her with her ear glued to the wire.

"Fire in the theater district," she said before Bitty could ask about Coalbank Hollow. "There is still heavy smoke in the area, and birds are advised to stay clear. In construction news, the capitol dome is almost complete, as is the world's tallest building, which will be opening in New York City. Meanwhile, back here in Charleston, the hawk population continues to rise."

"What about Coalbank Hollow?" Bitty asked, forcing the hawks from his mind.

"Most people don't ask for news from there," Walter said. "But I have some." She paused. "It isn't good."

Bitty's heart jumped to his throat, which was still sore from his cold. One look at the sparrow's face told him that the news was much more than Aunt Lou's arthritis acting up. "Go on."

Walter twitched her head to the right, then up toward the clouds. When she spoke, her voice was as smooth as a radio announcer's: "Two mining canaries, one male and one female, were killed early this morning in what is just the latest tragedy at the Coalbank Hollow mine. The canaries were found before the mine officially opened for the day, when they accompanied the fire boss on his morning rounds. The fire boss returned to the surface unharmed."

She looked at Bitty, her voice no longer smooth. "I'm sorry," she said. The wire seemed to sag even more with the weight of the news.

"Were there...did the report mention any names?" Bitty asked.

Walter twitched her head sideways again, then upright. "No names," she said. "It was an early report, quite fragmented, but our reporter stayed on the scene, so there's bound to be more later. Do you want me to see if—"

"No," Bitty said. "I'll check back."

So the full 103 days hadn't passed, but it didn't matter: he was still too late. He'd gone to the big city to try to change things and nothing had changed. Another accident. Another death. Two. *Two.* That part didn't make sense. Why had the Gap-Toothed Man taken two birds into the mine? Two birds, a male and a female, according to Walter's report. Alice and Chester? Uncle Aubrey and Aunt Lou? Bitty pictured the bird cemetery with two more sticks, and two more funerals he would never attend.

Alice's words came back to him. *"You could change things."*

"I have to see Eck," Bitty said.

"Maybe you should take a break," Clarence told him. "Come back to the station. We could—we could have a service here, if you want to."

Bitty shook his head. He wasn't going to grieve until he knew exactly who he was grieving for, so he could do it good and proper. "The best way to remember them is to make things better," he said. "I'm going to the inn."

"I don't think I could fit through the tunnel," Clarence said. "But I'll wait outside if you need me."

"No. I'll meet you back at the station," Bitty said. "I can do it alone."

"Are you sure?"

"I'm fine," Bitty said. But he wasn't.

He found Eck in the dining room. The mouse had a bandage that covered his eye and the wound above it, but the scratch on his rear was nearly healed.

"You look like a pirate from one of Jamie's books," Bitty said, forcing his voice to be light.

"*Arrrh!*" shouted Eck. "And you still look a bit under the weather, my friend."

Bitty thought about repeating Walter's news report, but he didn't want to talk about it. Besides, there wasn't time.

"Look sharp," Eck whispered. "Yon scallywag approaches." The second-floor house cat, who already looked thinner than the last time Bitty had seen him, tiptoed into the room.

"Very pleased with his progress," the mouse said. "Very pleased indeed."

The cat hadn't seen them yet, and Bitty felt the urge to do something reckless. He stepped out in the open and tried to think of something to say. He hadn't gotten very far in his studies with Miss Mona, but he cleared his throat and mustered the biggest meow he could. "*Hello!*" he shouted in distinct Cat. "*Where is the bathroom?*"

His accent wasn't perfect, but he could tell that Eck understood him from the way the mouse was laughing. The cat stopped, stretched and pointed with one paw in the general direction of his litter box. Bitty didn't follow the cat's directions. Instead he raced with Eck back into the mouse hole, as the cat made a half-hearted lunge.

"Did you hear me?" Bitty said, as he followed Eck through the tunnels, to Virgil Smith's downstairs room. "I talked to a cat!"

If only he could talk to Virgil Smith as easily. The inventor sat on his bed, tinkering with wires and tubes that were once again piled upon his nightstand.

"He's been working for hours," Eck said. "Comes out for meals and then starts working again. I think he's almost done."

The mechanism looked much the way it had earlier, before the cat had smashed into the table.

Bitty wanted a closer view. He popped out of the mouse hole and entered the room without even checking for cats. He cleared his throat.

"*Fee-yo.*" The inventor gave him the same intense look the politician had given him. But again, the man was no mind reader. Or was he?

Bitty hopped atop the table, and the man picked up something bright yellow and waved it at him: Bitty's tail feather.

"Yours, I presume?"

"*Fee-yo.*"

"I thought so."

Bitty was quiet.

"Interested in what I'm doing?" the man asked. "I presume you would be. This here's a gas detector. You might say this is your competition. Or would be, if I could ever sell it."

He smiled and turned out his pockets, which were empty. "They cost too much for me to produce just on spec," he said. "And I reckon I'm not much of a salesman. I don't know the right people."

Bitty wasn't much of a salesman, either. But he might know the right person. Plan E. He hadn't been in time to save Boggs, or the last two birds who had died in the No. 7, rest their souls. But those canary deaths were going to be the last. For the first time since stumbling out of his sickbed, Bitty knew exactly what he needed to do next.

He followed Eck back through the maze of tunnels. "Plan E," he said aloud.

"Ah," said Eck. "For *ergo*, no doubt."

"Ergo?"

"Meaning 'therefore,'" Eck told him. "You help the miners, *ergo,* they'll help you. Plan E."

When Bitty arrived back at the station, the pigeons were waiting for him, their faces so full of pity that the first thing he wanted to do was leave again. Work would keep him busy. He needed more newspaper. He wasn't hungry, but he needed food to bolster his strength. There was also his nest to rebuild—Clarence's mother wouldn't let him keep the hat.

"Bad luck to sleep there, surrounded by all those germs," she said. "You'd best start fresh."

Bitty flew from his thoughts. Once again, he gathered sticks and cotton and a patch of flannel from a workingman's shirt. He circled the building until he found a nook under an awning, safe from the rain and just one floor down from the pigeons. Clarence's mother approved. "If I were building a nest," she said, "that's just where it would go."

On to his letter, then. But by five p.m., he'd only found two scraps with the words he needed: 8 *a.m.* and *capitol.* He'd had better luck finding food: the heel of a loaf of bread and part of a hot pretzel, golden brown and dotted with chunks of white salt.

At six, he returned to the station's roof. The pigeons returned to gazing at him sympathetically, especially Clarence. Bitty knew it was their job, but they made him feel worse instead of better. He heard a toot in the distance, as if the train were grieving with him, and he flew to the station's weathervane to watch it approach. Smoke cascaded over the engine like a veil.

Bitty stared into it. Then, through the veil, he could make out two tiny dots, a mixture of yellow and black, floating toward him from one of the boxcars. They could have been fireflies or bumblebees. But no, they were larger than that. Ghosts? They got closer still, and Bitty could see them for what they really were: two canaries, covered with coal dust. His pulse quickened. It seemed impossible, but even from this distance Chester was unmistakably Chester. And

Alice—how many times had Bitty stared at her when he thought she wasn't looking? They were free. They were here. And, most importantly, they were *alive*.

Bitty's heart filled with a warmth he hadn't felt since he'd left Coalbank Hollow. He hadn't gone home; home had come to him. Relief surged through his veins like blood.

"Haaallooooo!" he yelled, sailing skyward. "Haaallooooo!" he called again. "It's me! It's Bitty!"

The canaries flew toward one another and would have collided like the cellar mice had Bitty not arced upward and out of the way. Then he swooped back down again and they all swirled around together, a spinning circle of color over the long, dark train.

"You're here! You're here! You're here!" Bitty looped twice like a trick airplane. The others followed; they flapped and they soared and they laughed. Finally, when Bitty ran out of breath, he landed on the terra-cotta tiles of the station's roof, about ten feet from the pigeons, who were watching, their sympathy replaced by astonishment. His friends landed beside him, where they belonged. But the others...? Bitty forced himself to ask the question he'd been carrying with him since he'd heard Walter's news report.

"Who's dead?"

Just then, Walter herself appeared on the station roof.

"I had to tell you right away," she said. "The story from Coalbank has been updated, with one very important correction. The two canaries who were reported killed at the Number Seven mine did *not* die this morning."

"They didn't?" Bitty repeated. In just a couple of hours, the sun would set, but now the light was dawning.

"No, it was just the opposite," Walter said. "They *escaped* to *Charleston*." She studied Alice and Chester, asking a silent question. They nodded. "Oh, this is news. This is big news. I've got to put this on the wire right away. But I'll be back. I want an exclusive interview with all three of you."

"How about that?" Chester said. "We're famous!"

"Do you want to clean up before you meet your adoring fans?"

Bitty said. "Or would you rather have something to eat first? How is everybody at home? How's Jamie? You've got to meet—how did you get *out?*"

"I can't answer all those questions at once," Alice said, laughing. "But I wouldn't mind a bath, if you know where I can find one."

"Food for me," Chester said. "Who cares about being clean?"

But he followed Bitty and Alice to the creek behind the station and washed the dust off his face anyway. Bitty stood guard, but no one—neither hawk nor grackle—bothered them.

"Chow time," Chester said. "After that you can show us your farm."

"Farm?" Bitty said. "What farm?"

"You're living with pigs," Chester said. "That was the message. 'Living at Char depot with pigs.'"

It was Bitty's turn to laugh. "But 'pigs' means—"

"'Pigs' means me," said Clarence, who appeared on the rock as if from thin air.

The others stared at him.

"Right," Bitty said. "This is Clarence. He's the friend I was talking about."

"He's a *pigeon*," Chester said.

"That's right," Clarence said. "You want to make something of it?"

"But pigeons are—"

"Don't say it."

"Rats with—"

"I said don't say it." Clarence raised his voice.

"*Stop,*" Bitty said. This wasn't going well at all. "Chester didn't mean...And Clarence isn't...It's not like that. He and his mom took care of me when I was sick. Listen, can't we all just—"

Argh. Why couldn't Chester keep his mouth shut? At least until everybody got to know each other. Bitty thought Clarence would fly away to sulk, but his new friend wasn't budging.

"You were sick?" Alice asked, changing the subject.

"Just a cold," Bitty said. "It was no big deal."

"No big deal?" Clarence said. "He almost *died*, that's all."

"You almost what?" Alice said. "There's so much to tell. It seems like you've been gone a year." She turned to Clarence.

"I'm Alice," she said.

"Clarence," Clarence said. He turned to Chester. "And you are...?"

"This is Chester," Bitty broke in before his friend could say anything. "Now, come on. Let's eat."

He led them to his nest and his store of food, which the pigeons had respectfully left alone. "So what happened?" he asked. "You first. The last I heard, two canaries were dead. And then you two showed up."

"Yeah, you first," Clarence said, directing his attention to Alice and ignoring Chester. "I've heard all Bitty's stories already."

They didn't need to be asked again. Between bites of the soft pretzel, Alice and Chester began telling the story of their escape from the Big House, which was every bit as exciting as Bitty's own.

Chapter 16

"Al can start. Ladies first and all that," Chester said, his mouth full.

So Alice began: "I guess it started when we found out you were safe. A blackbird brought us your message. He hollered the news right through Jamie's window. 'To all canaries present.' It was the first time we'd ever gotten a message from the outside. Aunt Lou nearly passed out. Anyway, the blackbird said you were safe and living 'at Char depot with pigs.' Of course we figured out you meant Charleston right away. As for the pigs part—"

"Oink," Clarence said.

"It's an abbreviation," Bitty explained. "I never thought you'd believe I was living with real pigs."

"Maybe it's best for Uncle Aubrey that we did believe it," Alice said. "Anyway, we knew you were safe and had started work. You have started work, right?"

"Yeah," said Chester. "What about your 'mission'?"

"You finish your story first," Bitty said. He wasn't quite ready to tell them what he'd accomplished so far—and what he hadn't. Unless he showed them a new bill that made it illegal to use canaries in coal mining, it wouldn't be good enough for Chester. And unless humans recognized canaries as heroes, it wouldn't be good enough for Uncle Aubrey.

"Well, Jamie got a canary to replace you," Alice said. "Bascom. He was so nervous; he passed out before the Gap-Toothed Man even took him into the mine for the first time. Then Uncle Aubrey had a close call—he passed out for real when he hit a pocket of bad air. Aunt Lou was so worried she nearly went bald. But Uncle Aubrey got better eventually, *and* he got to add two more marks to his perch. That made him impossible. 'Saving lives.' You know how he is. By then, Chester and I were sure we'd be better off out here with you. We started dreaming up all kinds of plans, and then Chester came up with a really good one."

Bitty had just enough time to wish that he'd been the one to get Alice out of the Big House instead of Chester and Chester's great plan. Then Chester took over.

"We didn't exactly *escape* from the Big House," he said. "We got kicked out."

"You got fired?" Bitty asked.

"Yup."

"I wonder what Uncle Aubrey thought about that!"

"I'm sure he was furious," Alice said. "You know how he is about our reputation. Anyway, you're messing it up, Ches; you have to start earlier."

Walter flew back to the roof in time to hear Chester begin again: A few days after Bitty left, after Bascom and Uncle Aubrey had already passed out, the Gap-Toothed Man snagged Chester and toted him down to good ol' No. 7.

"There were hardly any lights," Chester said, more to impress Clarence and Walter, who didn't know every detail, than Bitty, who did. "Those are the kinds of conditions *some of us* have to work in. The walls had a spooky glow."

There had been gas in the mine, just as there had been for Uncle Aubrey. It had gone straight to Chester's head. He shook and fluttered his wings. Then he fell backward with his legs in the air, as good as dead. The Gap-Toothed Man ran with him to the elevator and rushed him out into the cool, clean air.

"I woke up feeling like I'd taken a nine-pound hammer straight to the head," Chester said. But besides that, it was as if nothing had gone wrong at all. Chester was younger than Uncle Aubrey, and he recovered quickly. The miners lost a few hours of work; Chester was sent back to the Big House to rest. He had rested for about two days when the Gap-Toothed Man took him into the mine again.

"As soon as we entered the mine, I started squawking and flapping and I flopped on my back," Chester said. "Only this time? There wasn't any gas.

"The Gap-Toothed Man picked up the carrier and ran again," Chester continued. "He runs like an elephant." Once they were outside the mine, Chester stood up and pretended to be woozy. The miners went home for a couple of hours. And Chester got another day of rest.

After that, it became a game. Two days in a row, Chester volunteered for scouting duty. Each time, he passed out. The Gap-Toothed Man ran from the mine as if there were a tiger in it. The miners started grumbling—they only got paid for the coal they mined, and they couldn't mine much in half a day. Most of them weren't earning more than twenty dollars a week, at best. The big shots grumbled. Production was down. And the Gap-Toothed Man lost four pounds from the running he was doing.

"That's when he started to catch on," Chester said. "The next time he came looking for a scout, he took two of us."

Two mining canaries, one male and one female...

The miner's plan was to see if the two birds reacted the same way inside the mine. "But I saw that one coming a mile away. I told Alice that if he ever asked for two, she had to volunteer. If we both played dead and stayed dead, he'd open the cage and then we could break out. And if he didn't, well, we could always bite somebody, like a certain bird I know."

So that morning, when the Gap-Toothed Man reached his hand into the Big House, Chester flew into it. When the hand came back a second time, Alice flew into the line of fire.

"My mother yelled her head off," Alice said. "And I started to panic. I hadn't even practiced fainting."

Into the elevator they went, and down into the mine. When the doors opened, Chester started squawking. "Do what I do!" he yelled. They reached a bend in the mine and he flopped over with his eyes shut. Alice flapped and squawked and flopped.

"Al turned out to be a first-class fainter," Chester said. "A real natural."

"I *was* good," said Alice. "The Gap-Toothed Man took us up and out of there and into the coal yard."

"That must be when the reporter spotted you," Walter said.

"It must be," Alice said. "But then I messed up. I opened one eye—just one—and he was staring at me."

"*Fakers!*" the Gap-Toothed Man roared. "Troublemakers, that's what you are."

"He opened the cage," Alice said. "'Get out of here. *Scat.*' So we opened our eyes and flew into the morning."

"Were you scared?" Bitty asked.

"Who, me?" Chester said. "No way."

"I was," Alice said. "But I kept thinking about what you said. How could the real world be any scarier than it was in there?"

She took a bite of pretzel before Chester could finish it all. "The world seems pretty good, so far."

"How's everyone at home?" Bitty asked as Walter flew off again to add to her exclusive report.

"Aunt Lou and Uncle Aubrey are good," Alice said. "But do you remember that little green bird, the one that belonged to Mr. Paulowski?"

"Schwartzy?"

"He died the day after you left. And then there's Jamie." Alice's voice carried a current of sadness.

"He's not sick, is he?"

"No, but he and his dad have been fighting. Every night, it seems like."

"About the mine." It wasn't a question.

"Jamie says he won't work there," Alice said. "Not ever. But Mr. Campbell says there aren't any other jobs in Coalbank Hollow, and probably never will be. And that it's good work. 'Not to mention it's kept us all fed.'"

"What's his ma say?"

"She wants him to stay in school, go to college, even. But Mr. Campbell says they shouldn't entertain 'foolish notions.'"

For the first time since his friends had arrived, there was silence. They all wished they could change Clayton Campbell's mind. They wished they could help Jamie.

The birds kept talking as the sun set. Bitty told the story of his arrival in Charleston with more detail than ever before. His friends' beaks opened wide when he spoke in his limited Cat, and wider when he told them he'd seen Cipher, though it had been days since the hawk had shown herself. He told them everything: about his visit to the courthouse, his visit to the inventor and the breaking of the new-and-improved gas detector. He told them about his cold and about his last meeting with Delegate Finch. Alice sounded impressed. Chester didn't, but something—perhaps the salt in the pretzel—melted at least some of his sarcasm. Clarence drifted off to sleep, snoring softly, his head buried in his neck. Minutes later, they were all asleep, with Bitty sandwiched between his new friend and his two old ones.

Chapter 17

The next morning, Bitty woke and stretched. *Fffft.* His right wing brushed against the sleeping Chester, just like in the old days. But unlike the old days, he took a few tentative steps and then zoomed out from under the awning. Soon he was touching nothing but sky. He passed over Grackle Creek and glanced down at his reflection. He looked different than he had the last time he had studied himself: a small, scared bird, black with coal dust. He looked stronger.

When he returned from his flight, the station was crowded with people. He thought about Jamie's oatmeal breakfast as he scavenged the remains of an abandoned waffle. He flew with the pieces, one by one, and heaped them beside Chester and Alice.

"Wake up," he called. "We've got work to do."

Chester covered his eyes with his wings, but Alice hopped up and looked around.

"Where's Clarence?"

"He's got work to do, too," Bitty said.

"Ha!" Chester said from beneath his wings. "I thought you said he was a *pigeon*."

"Lay off, Ches," Bitty said. "We were dead wrong about the pigeons. Besides, he saved my life. Twice."

"Uncle Aubrey says—"

"Uncle Aubrey says a lot of things."

"Well, I think Clarence is nice," Alice piped up.

"Nice and touchy," Chester said, yawning. "Is that breakfast?"

"Yup."

"Why didn't you say so!" Chester rubbed the sleep out of his eyes and began to eat. While he munched, Bitty talked about plan E.

"For *Ergo*." He gave them Eck's definition.

"How's his gas detector better than us? Or anything else that's already out there."

"It's got a better alarm system, for one thing," Bitty said. "The inventor called it 'revolutionary.' Look, we help the miners, the miners help us. It's simple logic. All we have to do is talk to the right people."

"We don't know any people," Alice said. "Except the Campbells."

"And that politician I was telling you about."

"And I've been telling you," Chester said. "What has the government ever done for us?"

"But this guy is a *bird lover*," Bitty said. "Look, if I can get these guys together, I'm sure something will happen. Something *good*."

"And if I had a longer neck, I'd be a giraffe," Chester said.

"We flew here to be with Bitty," Alice said. "Let's hear him out."

"In other words—"

"In other words: Shut up." Bitty's eyes opened wide. He'd never heard Alice talk like that before. She looked at him. "What do you want us to do?"

So far Bitty's plans hadn't been exactly military operations. But this time he was sure of himself. "We need newspaper," he said. "We need to find words that humans can understand."

Bitty wasn't quite sure Mr. Finch would understand one of his crude notes, even if he *was* a bird lover. But Mr. Smith had an imagination.

Clarence came flying up, winded as usual. "Pete's gone," he said.

"What do you mean, gone?"

"He's not on his bench. He's not under his tree."

"Maybe he's just in the breadline," Bitty suggested. "Maybe he went for a walk."

"He's *gone*," Clarence said. "I can prove it."

They flew to the maple, where they found Pete's newspaper, neatly folded, resting against the trunk like a present. No doubt about it: the hobo had moved on to find some new stories, just as he'd said. Bitty hoped they'd be good ones. "I guess he won't mind if we borrow his paper, then." He wouldn't dream of cutting up the paper if Pete needed it. But if he didn't. . .

"He'd have given it to you himself, if he'd known," Clarence said.

"Are you okay?" Bitty knew Pete was the pigeon's favorite client.

"I guess." Clarence wobbled his head in something of a nod. "Well. Back to work."

Chester rolled his eyes. But as they turned the wrinkled pages of the newspaper, searching for words that were smooth enough to use, Bitty saw him look up to study the pigeons. Then he looked down again.

They had nearly every word they needed right in one spot, thanks to Pete. If they could find a scrap of paper to stick them on, they'd be set.

The downtown had the most potential, and Bitty wanted his friends to see what life was like on the other side of the river. They took off, near the trestle as always. But a gust of wind made them veer over the rushing water. "We should have read the flying report!" Chester hollered, his face wild and bright.

Bitty, whose mouth was full of newspaper, couldn't answer.

They flew past Capitol Drug, the hotel and the bank before they found a receipt outside the hardware store. It was mostly blank and carried an air of legitimacy; it would do. Bitty didn't know what the afternoon weather called for, and he wasn't going to take a chance on the rain. Again, using pinesap, he attached his words to the scrap of paper, clipping off *ings* and adding the occasional *s* and *ly*. His new note read as follows:

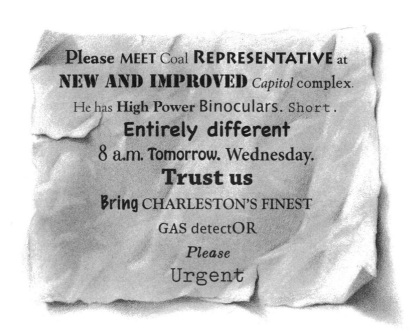

Please MEET Coal **REPRESENTATIVE** at
NEW AND IMPROVED *Capitol* complex.
He has **High Power** Binoculars. Short.
Entirely different
8 a.m. Tomorrow. Wednesday.
Trust us
Bring CHARLESTON'S FINEST
GAS detectOR
Please
Urgent

The *Charleston's finest* was Alice's idea—she thought if they paid the inventor a compliment, he'd be more likely to come. And it reminded them of their birdseed, back home. They found the word *gas* in an advertisement for Mister Lister's Sour Stomach Solver. And Bitty thought the extra *please* couldn't hurt.

They delivered the invitation quickly, carrying the paper through the tunnels and trying not to get it dirtier than it already was. Eck and Bonnie had just started conducting a training session on the third floor, so Bitty couldn't make introductions, but they looked in on one of the downstairs cats, who was chasing his tail in the bathtub.

Virgil Smith wasn't in his room. But Bitty saw three of the new gas detectors lined up beside the bed. With the help of his friends, Bitty placed the invitation on the man's nightstand, where his own tail feather still rested. He thought, for a second, about taking it back. But he left it where it was.

They headed home with a sense of accomplishment.

Now, if Mr. Smith would just find the note and then find Mr.

Finch and then—but that was too many ifs to think about. Bitty had his friends. He was free. And one of his plans was finally going right. Anything was possible.

They flew back down Virginia Street, trying to guess the number of rooms in each house they passed. As they turned onto Dickinson, they heard the rapid-fire chatter of a squirrel. He seemed to be repeating the same squeaky word over and over. Bitty had learned a number of words in Squirrel from his classmate and from Miss Mona. He recognized this one.

Hawk.

He repeated it, loudly, in a language Chester and Alice would understand. Already, they could make out the quiet beating of wings. There was a whoosh of air and a flash of talons.

One minute, Alice was flying beside him. The next minute, she was gone.

Chapter 18

"Alice!"

They screamed her name with one voice. Bitty didn't look at Chester, because that would make it real. He hesitated only a second. "Follow them!" he said.

The hawk was fast and had a head start, but she was flying for two. Her bent wing worked fine on the glides, but her flapping wasn't steady. The canaries were gaining.

"Where are they headed?" Chester yelled.

Bitty didn't know. And then he did.

"The river."

The hawk didn't appear to be worried that the canaries were behind her. Perhaps she was hoping they would follow so she could eat the three of them in order: breakfast, lunch and dinner. Bitty blamed himself. He'd known Cipher was out there, but he'd gotten comfortable. He hadn't been vigilant. He hadn't watched the skies.

The river loomed ahead of them, deep and wide. The hawk flew straight toward the open water and angled low, until Alice's tail feathers, then her head, went under. The hawk moved up and down over the current. Bitty watched as Alice gulped air, then water, then air again.

They had to act fast. Bitty spotted a stick floating downstream. He couldn't slash it like a pirate sword, but he and Chester might be able to manage it with their beaks. "Grab the other end!" he yelled.

"What are you trying to do?"

"Just grab it!" Bitty ordered. "There's no time!"

Perhaps it was all those years of sleeping in close proximity. Perhaps it was their time together in the mine, communicating with waves and taps. Chester picked up the other end of the stick in his beak. Together, he and Bitty lifted it and flew to face the hawk. Cipher's hulking body dwarfed the canaries. Bitty felt smaller than he ever had. For a split second, the killer seemed to regard them both, menacing but amused, as if they were the main entertainment and Alice, barely struggling now, was the opening act.

Bitty and Chester flew toward the hawk at full speed and caught her in the neck with their stick. Their combined force was enough to knock the breath out of her, and for one moment she loosened her grip on Alice. They dropped the stick and grabbed their friend instead, steering her to a rock that jutted out of the current. Water bubbled from her beak as the hawk fell into the rushing river. The current carried her a short distance, but then she was out of the water again. Angry now, she twisted her head to the right, then the left, and regarded the three birds with a calculating eye. "*Fee. Fi. Fo. Fum.*"

Then they heard another sound, which to Bitty was chillingly familiar. "Chck. Chck. Watch it."

"Now what?" Chester asked.

"You don't want to know," Bitty told him.

The taunt came again. "Chck. Chck. Watch it." Bitty looked up in time to see V, the leader of the grackles, begin his torpedo attack. The canary flashed back to his first Charleston morning, and the way the water had numbed his feet while fear numbed everything else. *Well, let him come,* he thought. *Let them all come.* Bitty wasn't hiding this time. He might be hawk food or grackle food, but he wasn't going down without a fight.

The other grackles joined V in the downward plunge, and Bitty braced for the attack. He squared his shoulders, and he didn't close his eyes. Then he saw that the grackles were not aiming for him. They weren't aiming for Alice or Chester, either. It was the *hawk* they were threatening.

They buzzed around Cipher's head the way they had buzzed around Bitty that day at the creek. They swirled and pecked and taunted until the hawk turned her regal body away from the water, flapped her wings twice and glided toward the shore with V and the Boys swarming behind her.

Chapter 19

"I never thought I'd be grateful to the grackles for anything," Bitty told Clarence when Alice had dried out enough to make it back to the train station. They'd settled her in Bitty's nest and she'd gone to sleep instantly, bruised but alive.

"Hawks eat grackles, too," Clarence pointed out. "Lucky you had a common enemy."

"Yeah," Bitty said. "Lucky."

Alice still ached when they awoke the next morning.

"You stay here," Bitty said. "Chester and I will go the capitol. We'll tell you everything that happens."

"Don't forget me," Clarence said. "Unite! Plan E. I'm a part of this mission, too."

"So am I," Alice said.

"Alice—"

"I'm going with you," she said. "You can't stop me."

They didn't try.

They flew slowly, resting often—once halfway across the bridge. Bitty and Chester spent so much time watching the sky, they never saw the water. Clarence, with his spastic flight rhythm, flew just above them or just below them, daring anyone else to get close.

By the time they reached the site of the new capitol building, Virgil Smith was there, standing by the rock where the two birdwatchers sat, same as last time, overlooking the river. The inventor wore a rumpled shirt and tie but no jacket. He clutched his gas detector in both hands, as if it were a baby instead of a piece of machinery.

The birds flew close enough to listen.

"—even afford it?" Mr. Finch was saying. "Tough times, after all."

The men descended into silence, and Bitty shook his head. Had they come this far to watch the whole plan dissolve? He didn't have a plan F. He didn't want to make one.

"I'll tell you what," Mr. Finch said finally. "I'm heading back to my district in the morning. Just how many of those things do you have finished?"

"About half a dozen, sir. But I can work on a bigger scale if I get a little seed money."

"Why don't you bring them, all of them, and come along? If you can convince the mine in Coalbank to try them out, *I'll* figure out a way to pay for them. Heck, Noble here's a financier," Mr. Finch said, indicating the man beside him. "Maybe we could talk him into chipping in. That'll get you your seed money."

"Yep," Noble said.

"That's awful kind," said Virgil Smith. "And I'd be mighty obliged. But why would you do that?"

Mr. Finch lifted his binoculars like a torch. "I'm a bird lover," he said. "And my brother was a doctor at a coal camp once. Besides, it isn't often a politician gets to be a hero. Is it?"

Mr. Finch rose to his feet and shook the inventor's hand.

"Would you mind telling me something?" asked Mr. Finch.

"No, sir."

"How did you even know where to find me this morning? Session's over."

Mr. Smith reached into his pocket and pulled out Bitty's tail feather. "A little bird told me," he said.

The birds didn't speak as they flew back across the rushing river. They landed near Mrs. Gillespie's bench so Clarence could make up for his morning off.

"So we have to go back," Alice said finally.

"Of course we do," Bitty said. "I don't want to find out about whatever happens from a news report. But I'll miss this place."

"Wait, you're leaving?" Clarence said. "All of you?"

"Plan E," Bitty said. "The mission's only partially accomplished. We have to see it through."

"Shortest vacation in history," Chester said. "It wouldn't even get a mention in the Coalbank paper." He made his voice as snooty as possible: "'Coalbank canaries Chester and Alice visited their friend Bitty, who resides at the Charleston train station, for a lousy forty-eight hours.'"

Though it was clear he didn't want to give Chester the satisfaction, Clarence laughed.

"I wish you could come with us, Clarence," Bitty said. "Just to visit."

"I'm not much of a flier."

"Aw, you could make it. All we've got to do is catch the train. After that, it's a smooth ride."

"Supposing I did go," Clarence said. "What would we eat?"

"For crying out loud," said Bitty. "We'll find something. We always do. Just come."

"Yeah. Come," Chester added.

Clarence looked at Chester. "Are you sure the hawk didn't dunk *you* underwater?"

"I don't need a hawk to tell me I've been a jerk," Chester said. "Come with us. Bitty needs a bodyguard."

"I'm not that much smaller than you," Bitty said.

"Well," said Chester. "Maybe we all need one."

"Have you ever seen any pigeons in Coalbank Hollow?" Clarence asked.

"No. But you've got to remember, we didn't get out much."

Finally, Clarence agreed. The next step was to ask his mother for permission.

"I won't be gone long," Clarence said.

"But you'd have to come back all by yourself," she said, wobbling her head in what looked like a no. "I don't want you flying alone."

"Bitty flew alone, and he's a lot smaller than me."

"Bitty didn't have a choice," she said. "But I wonder... Your aunt Zelda's in Oak Hill. It's been a long time since we've had a visit. What if I went with you partway? You could fly on to Coalbank Hollow and then, after your visit, come back to meet me. I've always wanted to ride a train."

"We'll do it!" Clarence said before she could change her mind.

Bitty went in search of Miss Mona. He wanted to send a message home so the other canaries would know they were coming. When he got to the snaky black wire, though, Miss Mona wasn't there. Instead, standing sentry, was one of V's boys, a fierce-looking yellow-eyed grackle.

The phone wire barely shook when Bitty landed on it. The grackle turned, staring at him over the tip of his pointy black beak.

"I need to send a message to Coalbank Hollow, please," Bitty said quickly. "To Two One Two Slusser Road. You can address it to 'all canaries present.' Tell them I'm coming home."

The grackle stood as still as the snarling lions that watched over the train station. When he spoke, he wheezed like a broken squeak toy. "You're leaving?"

"For a while," Bitty said. "So if you could just send the message."

"Coming home," the grackle repeated. "Got it."

"Thank you," Bitty said. "For the message and... for earlier. For the hawk."

The grackle didn't say anything, and Bitty turned to leave.

"Chck, chck," the grackle called. "Watch it." From the bird's dark countenance, it was impossible for Bitty to judge whether the grackle was making fun of him or wishing him a safe journey. The bird lowered his raspy voice. "Happy to help the cause," he added. "But don't tell anyone. It would ruin our reputation."

Bitty spent the rest of the afternoon flying around the city. He tried to call on Eck to say good-bye, but the mouse was nowhere to be found. If the mines had taught him one thing, it was the value of a true friend. He'd seen it among the men who worked together and relied on one another. He'd seen it in the Big House. And now he'd seen it here. Bitty searched room after room for the mouse. He couldn't find Bonnie, either. He didn't want to leave without seeing them one last time, but after an hour's wait, he left a message with the cellar mice. He didn't expect them to deliver it.

Back at the station, he found Clarence's mother pacing on the pavement beneath his nest. "Are you going to take it apart or leave it the way it is?" she asked.

"I'll leave it," Bitty decided. "I'll come back. And in the meantime, some other bird might need it." He stood for a moment as the sun began to set, trying to remember every detail he could about his station, his nest and his city.

"If you're done here," Clarence's mother said, "there are some folks who are waiting to say good-bye."

Bitty followed her to the balcony, lit by the fading sun and the glow from the familiar arched windows. He landed to the cheers of his new friends. All the pigeons were there. And there was Eck! And Bonnie! So this was where they had been hiding. He took his place beside them. They had brought several servings of the Gilmer Inn's famous corn bread, though the sparrows gobbled it down before Bitty got even a crumb. Gladys and Phil, the seagulls, were there, too, with a tin of smelly sardines. Dolly, the chimney swift who had called him "sugar," was there. So were Walter and Miss Mona and the squirrel and the cardinals from Bitty's language class. His old friends were there, smiling beside him. And strangers were there—creatures who had heard about his mission and wanted to feel they were a part of it.

The clouds faded from orange to dusty pink, then disappeared into the coming night. Everyone ate and drank and told stories. Some mourning doves dropped by and sang, and Eck and Bonnie demonstrated the dances they'd seen in the inn's drawing room: a waltz and the Lindy Hop. "I'd like to propose a toast," Eck said. "To Bitty: a brave adventurer and a fine friend. And to a mission accomplished!"

To a mission half accomplished, Bitty thought. He opened his beak as if to make a speech, but the only words he could free from his throat were "Thank you . . . I'll miss you all."

"We'll miss you," Miss Mona told him, in Squirrel, Bird and Armadillo. "Don't worry; we'll tell your story to everyone we see."

The squirrel nodded. So did Eck. "Communication," he said. "Public awareness of the plight of our fellow creatures. That's what it's all about. "

The hour grew late. One by one, Bitty's friends departed. *"Eeni,"* he told Eck, touching the mouse on the shoulder with his wing. "I would never have made it here if it hadn't been for you."

"Eeni," Eck said. He smiled, curled his tail like a lasso and twirled it. "You would have made it. You're a survivor."

Now familiar with the train's schedule, the canaries decided to take the noon special so that the pigeons could fit in one last morning shift at the park. Soon they were poised on the roof and ready to go. They heard the train before they saw the big black engine barreling toward them.

Tooooooooot.

They waited for it to slow and stop. Instead, it whistled past them, heading south. If they didn't catch up with it soon, it would hit the tunnel the coal trains used as a shortcut. Bitty and Chester took off as fast as they could, with Alice, who was still slower than usual, behind them. A little farther back came Clarence's mother, huffing and puffing, and behind her flapped Clarence. His strange flying rhythm had once made Bitty laugh. Now it made him panic. Clarence moved in spurts, burping his way through the sky. He'd sink low, then soar, then sag back down.

"It's his stomach!" yelled Alice as the canaries reached the train's red caboose and found their footing on the guardrail. *"Come on, Clarence, you can do it!"*

"I'm . . . coming," Clarence called. He wasn't coming fast enough.

Clarence's mother reached the caboose, too breathless to speak. They neared the mouth of the tunnel. If Clarence didn't make it soon, he'd be lost in the darkness, with no hope of catching up.

"Hurry!" Bitty yelled. *"Faster!"*

Clarence was concentrating too hard to reply.

"Flap. Flap. Flap," Bitty yelled in rhythm with the train's wheels.

Alice and Chester joined in, along with Clarence's mother: "One, two, three. *Flap. Flap. Flap.*"

Clarence flapped. The burping eased and his rhythm evened out. He pushed ahead in a final burst of speed just as the rear of the train disappeared into the blackness of the tunnel. Bitty felt, more than he saw, Clarence land on the caboose beside him.

They rode on, listening to the chug of the wheels and the panting of the pigeons. Soon they could see shadows again. Then the train chugged back into the brightness of the early afternoon.

Scenery whizzed by. Now Bitty was able to see the country he had missed during his dark, sleepy ride northeast. He could see the mountains stacked behind each other, blue, like waves. The train snaked along beside them and through them, passing towns and valleys and gaps. At each station, the train paused just long enough for a hiccup. As they approached Oak Hill, Clarence's mother bobbed her head at them. "Be careful, now, all of you," she said. "Remember, our aunt Zelda is your aunt Zelda. You know where to find me! Oh, dear, I'd better hurry before I—" A flutter of feathers, and she was gone.

On they went, toward Coalbank Hollow. The train stopped briefly to change drivers, and the friends (except for Clarence, who decided he was better off where he was) left the caboose to hunt for food. The muscles in Bitty's wings were strong now. There was no ache as he zipped through the bushes and snatched a teaberry he found growing low to the ground.

The train started again, and soon Bitty recognized the mountains as his own. "This is it," he announced. "Everybody off." He led the way toward the coal camp he had seen whole only once before. He and Chester jockeyed for position, each vying for the role of tour guide.

"On your right you will see some company houses," Bitty said.

"On your left you will see more company houses," said Chester.

Outside one of them, a group of children played tag in the warmth of the afternoon.

"On your right is the company store," Bitty announced as they flew past the window. The display had changed since March, and now it featured pots, pans, medicines, pickaxes, a red wagon that looked identical to the canaries' former chariot, and a doll with real hair. "This is where the miners spend their paychecks before they even get their paychecks."

"They carry our birdseed," Chester added. "Not that I eat that stuff anymore."

They came upon a tiny building Bitty hadn't noticed the last time through. One side of the shingle said medical office. The other side said vet. Hanging on the door was a piece of paper with writing that was almost illegible. *Boy needed,* it said. *See Doc.*

"We'd better take it," Chester said. "For Jamie."

They grabbed the note the same way they had grabbed the stick and lugged it to Jamie's house, which was right where they'd left it. They dropped the sign on the porch, to the right of the front door, where Mr. Campbell usually left his boots.

"We lived around back," Bitty told Clarence, flying to Jamie's bedroom window. Bitty used to spend all his time looking out that window. Now he was looking in. The cage was there, right next to Jamie's bed. Bitty thought it would be empty, and that the canaries would be at work. Instead, the cage was full.

Chapter 20

"So you're back, are you?" Uncle Aubrey's voice seared through the gap beneath the window. "Want your old jobs? Well, you're too late."

"Bitty, thank goodness you're safe!" said Aunt Lou.

"Wait," Bitty said. "I don't understand. Why are you all here?"

"Gas detectors," Uncle Aubrey said. "'Innovative.' 'Better.' They got here last night. Some fancy-pants politician swept into town and talked the boss man into trying them out. Foreman comes by and says, 'You give those birds a rest tomorrow, Clay.' Says some inventor's got something special, a mechanical canary.

"Mr. Campbell says, 'I've seen them things before. I'll stick with my bird, thank you very much.' Foreman says, 'You've got to set an example, Clay. You bring your bird, it just won't look right. It'll look like you're second-guessing the management.'"

"But that doesn't make any sense," Bitty said. "How could they have gotten here so soon?"

Uncle Aubrey glared. "This was your doing? Was this how you were going to make things 'better' for everybody? By putting us all out of work?"

Bitty's silence amplified his guilt. Uncle Aubrey shifted his rage to Alice and Chester. "Of course they'd welcome a *machine*, after dealing with the likes of you two," he said. "Getting fired. You've ruined our reputation. Ruined it." He sounded like the grackle.

"Careful, Aubrey. That's my daughter you're talking to right there," said Alice's mother.

Uncle Aubrey's eyes moved farther down the window ledge. There was only one bird he hadn't addressed yet, and it wasn't a canary.

"A pigeon?" said Uncle Aubrey, who had apparently seen one before. "You can't be serious."

"This is Clarence," Bitty said. "My friend."

"Well, that figures."

"Aubrey." Aunt Lou's voice was full of needles. "Be quiet and let the kids talk." She looked through the bars at her nephew. "There, now. Tell us everything."

They did, taking turns, even Clarence.

"Languages," Uncle Aubrey sputtered when they were done. "Telephones. Grackles. Mice who speak Bird. It's all Squeak to me, that's what I say. And pigeons." He looked at Clarence. If canaries had been able to spit, Uncle Aubrey would have. "Pigeons. *Working.* Is that what you want me to believe?"

"Uncle Aubrey, everyone knows that—" Bitty began, with a worried glance at his friend, though this time, Clarence looked more amused than offended.

"A waste of wings, if you ask me," Uncle Aubrey said. "Though I guess I didn't do anything with my own wings today, now, did I?"

Trying to talk to Uncle Aubrey was like trying to talk to a lump of coal. No—it was worse. At least he could pretend that the coal was listening to him. Bitty looked at his family stuck behind the bars while his uncle ranted and raved. He needed air. Now. He shot up and over the roof and was rewarded for his decision: there was Jamie, walking up the road, his schoolbooks and baseball glove slung over his shoulder. The boy seemed to have grown the way everything does in spring. His brown hair was tucked back behind his ears; his pants hovered too far above his ankles. Bitty watched as Jamie climbed onto the uneven porch and picked up the note from Doc Tatum.

He dropped his books. "Ma!" he yelled. "I'm running to town.

I'll be back!" When he returned home thirty minutes later, he was whistling.

"*Fee-yo.*" Bitty swooped onto the porch and interrupted Jamie's tune. He worried that the boy wouldn't recognize him. He worried that he would.

"Big Yellow!" Jamie said. "You came home!" He grinned the way he did when Mrs. Campbell made apple pie. "Guess what?" the boy told him. "I've got a job. Well, maybe I do. Doc's going to try me out for a week because I've got experience with animals. And if I do a good job, he said he might let me help him out for the whole year. What do you think of that?" He gazed at the bird again. "Where have you been all this time? I must have checked every tree."

Warmed by the smile, Bitty flew in an orbit around Jamie's head. The boy watched him until his mother called from inside the house. "Don't go anywhere," Jamie said. "My ma won't believe this."

When the boy went inside, Bitty flew as far as the back ledge, to get another lecture from Uncle Aubrey and to wait for the return of Mr. Campbell and a report on the mechanical canaries.

The whistle blew, signaling the end of the shift. Bitty flew to the roof. The shingles felt rough beneath his feet, not smooth like the terra-cotta tiles on the train station. Mr. Campbell was walking home along the tracks, with the Gap-Toothed Man beside him. They were swinging their lunch pails like school boys.

"See you, Steve."

"Say hello to Mary."

"You tell Becca the same."

The free birds joined Bitty on the roof.

Thud. Thud.

"What was that?" Clarence said.

"Mrs. Campbell won't let him in the house until he takes off his boots."

A second later the door opened and shut. Bitty could hear the Campbells talking in the main room, and Jamie's footsteps as the boy ran to join them.

"Well? How'd they do?" Jamie asked.

"Finally taking an interest in the mine, are you?" said Mr. Campbell. "How'd who do?"

"Quit teasing, Pa. You know who I mean!"

"The mechanical canaries?" Mr. Campbell said. "Can't say as I felt completely comfortable, going in without a live bird. But a lot of the other miners seemed to like the idea, especially when that Delegate Finch said the new equipment comes without a price tag. If we don't have to pay for canaries, that's one less expense for us. And as he reminded us, 'These here won't die They won't get sick or eat sunflower seeds.' Said the mine could have them, no strings attached. Said they would give us a sense of—what was the word he used? Modernity. Safety and modernity. He's coming back in a couple of days to see how we like 'em."

Chester leaned over and whispered: "Can you imagine Uncle Aubrey after he's been out of work for a few days? Maybe we'd better go back to Charleston."

But they stayed.

The free birds set up a camp tucked away in the green needles of a cedar tree, while the rest of the canaries stayed crowded in the Big House. Uncle Aubrey was more like a lion than a bird; he roared whenever anybody tried to talk to him. Clarence had a hard time being out of work, too. The miners were gone all day, and the women walked too quickly from one thing to the next. Clarence tried following Mrs. Campbell around, but she almost kicked him twice when she hung out the laundry. He was forced to eat berries instead of bread.

On the brighter side, Clarence joined the canaries for a baseball game between the miners of Coalbank and the miners of McDowell (they cheered for Coalbank). And from their spot in the tree, they could hear the strains of music from front porch picking that seemed to be as much a part of the West Virginia night as the stars.

And then, two nights after the game, Mr. Campbell knocked on Jamie's bedroom door with an update. "It's official," he told his son. "They don't want your canaries anymore. They said it makes us look

too old-fashioned. It's time to join the twentieth century and let…
how did he put it? 'Let the innovations take over.' "

Uncle Aubrey swore. "Machines to a do a bird's job. Here of all
places. That tears it."

"At least they'll be safe now," Jamie said.

"Nobody's going to be paying you anymore to take care of those
birds, Jamie. You know that. You're going to have to come up with
the feed money yourself. Doc Tatum giving you anything for helping
him out this week?"

"Feed," Jamie said.

"Well, that's something. Listen. You can keep them birds if you
want to. Or you can let 'em go. I'm leaving that up to you."

He went back into the kitchen. The birds studied Jamie for a
sign of his decision, but they didn't get one. That night, before bed,
he stared into the canary cage for a long time. Bitty watched through
the window. He wished—for a second—that he were close enough
for the boy to touch his head.

"Oh, this is ridiculous," Chester's mother said from the cage.
"Our lives in the hands of an eleven-year-old boy?"

But their lives were always in someone's hands.

The next day, Jamie walked home from school with one of his
friends, a boy named Preach who was a year older and a head shorter.

"You wanna throw?" Preach said, tossing a baseball and catching it.

Jamie didn't answer, so Preach sat down on the bed and they both
stared at the birds.

"I know how they feel in there. *I know*," Jamie said. Bitty had
heard that once before and hadn't believed it. Maybe the boy did have
a clue after all.

"How do you mean?" said Preach.

"The mine's the only place to go in this town, and that's if we're
lucky." Jamie stared outside, through his bedroom window, and
started walking toward it. The canaries and Clarence, who were sitting on the ledge again, scattered, just in time.

BANG!

Jamie threw open the window, as wide as it would go.

Then he unlatched the door of the cage. Bitty could hear Aunt Lou squawking and Mrs. Campbell's voice saying, "Jamie? You sure, now?"

"I am," Jamie said. "Go," he told the birds.

One by one, the canaries of the Big House lit out of the cage, then out of the window, joining Bitty and his friends in the open air.

"Mission accomplished!" Bitty wanted to yell, but he didn't want to provoke Uncle Aubrey, who landed on Jamie's roof and stayed there, sulking, while the rest of the birds flew in circles, as if the freedom had made them drunk. The humans followed them outside and watched as the birds wove patterns of color across the sky.

Finally, the canaries followed Bitty to the cedar tree. Uncle Aubrey gave in and came with them, though he muttered the whole way. "Forced retirement. Displacement. It's better than being fired, but not by much."

"What are we supposed to do now?" wheezed Old Bird Crockett when they reached the tree. From a distance, they looked like lemons on the branches.

"Florida might be nice," Aunt Lou said. "Good for our joints, don't you think? And your lungs, too, Crock. I would so love to see the ocean."

"They use canaries in England, too, you know," Uncle Aubrey said. "Bet no one over there's been replaced."

"I want to *see* the ocean," Aunt Lou said. "I don't want to fly over it."

"If they can take a train," Uncle Aubrey said, glaring at Bitty, "then we can take a boat. This is our work we're talking about here."

"We could go back to Charleston," Bitty said. Clarence bobbed and nodded, but Uncle Aubrey fixed the pigeon with a cold, hard stare.

Bitty was about to jump to Clarence's defense—it looked as if the pigeon was the one who needed a bodyguard—when the tree trembled. For a split second after that, all of nature seemed to freeze. Then a sparrow came speeding through the coal camp. He shouted something to a squirrel, who shouted to the canaries as he ran past the cedar. Bitty scarcely needed to translate, but he did, just before the warning whistle blew: "It's the mine. Something's gone wrong at the mine."

Chapter 21

"You can bet those gas detectors were responsible," Uncle Aubrey said. "Using machines to do a bird's job. *Hmmph.*"

Bitty looked around, wildly, though there was nothing to see. If the new gas detectors were responsible, that meant *he* was responsible. He'd brought them here. He'd gotten the canaries out of the mine, but what had he done for the men? Plan E: help the miners, *ergo* the miners will help the birds. He seemed to have skipped the first part of that equation. He shuddered and said aloud what they all were thinking: "I hope Jamie's pa is safe."

Jamie and his mother were still standing in the yard with Preach. They looked toward the mine as if the answers to their questions would be written in smoke above it. A siren wailed, and they took off at a run. Bitty followed them. When he looked back, he saw the whole flock, a swarm of color, right behind him with Clarence, gray and reliable, in the rear. The Campbells kept running with Preach until they reached a pile of timbers near the entrance of the mine. The birds landed on top of it. Above them, the tipple was still and silent. Men had already risen from the shaft, their faces black, their eyes bloodshot, their hats in their hands. From the houses the women came running, their own faces as white as the moon. Jamie's mother clutched her apron strings as if they were holding her together.

"Bo?" she yelled, and Bitty recognized Bo Collins, the mine's foreman. Mr. Collins shook his head and kicked over a metal lunch pail. He walked to a square board where eleven silver disks—called checks—hung from nails. It looked like a child's game, but Bitty knew what it meant: eleven men were still inside. Mr. Collins reached for one of the disks and handed it to Jamie's ma. Twenty-seven, it said: Clayton Campbell's number.

Jamie's mother squeezed the disk so tight, it must have made an imprint in her hand. "I'm sorry, Mary," said the foreman. "I don't have anything else to tell you yet."

"Darn Steve and those cigars," one of the miners muttered.

"Slow down, Vincenzo, he's not stupid. He's never lit one before. Let's not go pointing fingers. Storm's brewing. It could just as well have been lightning. Or a rockfall."

"It could have been a spark from one of those mechanized canary doohickeys," said Rusty. The humans and canaries stood, together but apart, waiting for movement and answers.

"Where's the rescue team?" Jamie asked. His mother closed her eyes. Jamie stood next to her for a minute, then walked deliberately toward the mine. "I'm going to find them," he said.

"Jamie! You get back here this *instant*."

Mary Campbell's voice was drowned out by a Ford crunching over the gravel road, honking as it came. Two ambulances pulled in behind it, and a truck full of rescue workers with a baying blood-hound behind that.

"He'll probably get all of the headlines," Uncle Aubrey muttered. "Just watch."

Mrs. Campbell turned away to embrace Mrs. Albini, a neighbor, who stood taller because her husband was safe.

Jamie kept walking.

"He's going," Bitty whispered.

"What?" Clarence said.

"Jamie," Bitty said. "He's going into the mine."

"He's nuts," Chester said.

"It's still dangerous," Alice said, understanding.

"I'm going in," Bitty said. "If there's bad air in there, I can warn him. He can run."

"I'm going with you, Bitty," Alice said. It didn't bother him anymore that she hadn't found a nickname for him. Bitty. That was who he was.

"I'll come, too," Chester added. "It'll be better if there are three of us. I think."

Clarence cocked his head toward Jamie's mom. "I'll stay with her," he said. Uncle Aubrey looked at the pigeon. It was a warmer look than he'd given the bird earlier, but still full of suspicion.

"Good," Bitty said. He felt as if he should say something more, but he didn't know what.

"You don't have to go, you know," Clarence said.

"Yes," Bitty said. "I do."

"Well. If we're going, we'd better—" Chester began.

"Go now," Bitty finished. They flew together to the entrance of the mine. Jamie had already hit the lever on the elevator, which started its descent. Bitty and his friends ducked inside before it disappeared completely into the bowels of the mountain. They lit on a railing, as if it were their old perch.

It was strange, being in a cage again, even one as big as this. Bitty wondered if the others felt it, too, as Jamie turned on them with a light he had snagged from the coal yard.

"You want your old jobs back?" he asked. "Is that it?"

The elevator continued down the shaft. Finally, it hit bottom.

"If you're sure about this," Jamie said, stepping out of the lift, "stick close." The canaries took the lead, hovering just ahead of the boy. Down the main corridor they went. But there were so many turns and bends—the miners could be anywhere. They pressed on. The only sound was the dripping of water and the run-stop-stagger of Jamie's feet. And then they heard it. *Tink, tink, tink.* A tapping sound, muffled, as if it were coming from deep within a wall. "That's them," Jamie said, running. Then he stopped. His light shone on a pile of coal, rock and timber that reached from the ground to the mine's low roof. "The ceiling must have caved."

Jamie yelled: "Pa? Hello. Anyone? Can you hear me? Hello?"

The tinking sound stopped for a minute, then started again, faster.

"I can hear them!" Jamie yelled. *"I found them! I can hear them!"*

In time, they heard the distant shouts of the rescue crew, and Jamie kept yelling until the crew reached them.

"Son, what in the blazes are you doing here?" one of them asked. "You should be—"

"I hear them," Jamie said. "Listen."

They quieted. *Tink. Tink.*

"We'll have to dig for them," another man said, a mask covering his face and giving him air. "But we can't start now. You need to get out of here, son. Look: your birds."

Chester fell first. Bitty and Alice saw him drop to the ground like a dead leaf, his beak wide open. Alice opened her own beak to sound the alarm, but her lungs, too, filled with invisible, deadly gas. Bitty fell last. He kept his eyes open long enough to see the flame on Jamie's lamp glow orange, then blue. Jamie reached for him. Then Bitty saw nothing but black.

He awoke to find himself jiggling in Jamie's arms, just outside the mine's main entrance. A rescue worker was with them, holding the bloodhound by the leash.

"How in the Sam Hill—?" shouted Bo Collins, the foreman.

"Bad air," Jamie said, panting. "They're trapped. Rock fell, a lot of it, but they can't start digging yet."

The rescue worker nodded and lifted his mask.

"How long until you can get them?" Mr. Collins asked, but the man couldn't say.

Mr. Collins apparently forgot that Jamie shouldn't have been in the mine in the first place. "How are they?" he asked. "Could you tell?"

"They were tapping," Jamie said. "They're walled in. I don't know how much air they've got. I don't know if..."

Mr. Collins put a hand on Jamie's shoulder. "Just find your mother," he said. "They were tapping, you said?"

Jamie nodded.

"Hold on to that, then. Those taps."

Jamie walked to the edge of the coal yard and placed the three canaries in a patch of weeds.

Bitty still felt far away, as if it were all happening to someone else. Jamie's mother came to them, looking half-asleep. Clarence waddled behind her, double-time.

"You okay?" Clarence asked Bitty.

"I think so." Bitty's voice echoed inside his head.

"Are they?" Clarence asked.

Jamie leaned over Chester and Alice, massaging their tiny chests.

"Course we're okay," said Chester, though his voice was weak. "Just another day in paradise."

"Tough job you guys have here," Clarence said.

"You're heroes," Jamie whispered. "You know it?"

The words seemed to clear Chester's head. "Hear that?" he crowed loudly. "*Heroes.*"

The word made Bitty itch. "No one's made it out yet," he said.

"Jamie did," Chester told him. They all turned their attention back to the mine.

"How many lives?" Uncle Aubrey called. "How many lives did we save?"

"We don't know." Bitty's head was still throbbing. "We're waiting."

"Excellent job, my boy," Uncle Aubrey said, flying closer. "Good work. And you." He turned to the pigeon, standing at attention at Mrs. Campbell's feet, and cleared his throat. "Clarence," he said, using the bird's name for the first time. "Good work."

An hour passed. Two. Five. Women arrived carrying stew and pumpkin bread, but the food brought little comfort. Even the ambulance drivers, who stood away from the rest, only had coffee. The birds didn't eat, either—not even Clarence.

Mr. Finch arrived, along with Virgil Smith, who twisted a small piece of wire in shaky hands. "If it was my invention," he said. "If it caused a spark, if there was some kind of malfunction..."

"Then we'll both be ruined," Mr. Finch finished. "Let's not get ahead of ourselves. Let's not jump to conclusions."

Darkness fell and people prayed, their many voices merging into one.

Mr. Finch walked among them, talking and listening as the miners spoke of weak support beams, thick coal dust, long hours and lousy ventilation. Mrs. Polly was there, the widow of the man who'd died with Boggs. She'd received no compensation and just a sliver of his last paycheck. The mine hadn't even paid for his burial. She gave Mr. Finch an earful.

"When this is over," Mr. Finch said, "I'm going to see what we can do to improve this situation. I am." He was speaking to the miners, but Bitty thought he was speaking to the canaries, too, even if he wasn't using his bird whistle this time.

More praying. Rescuers moved in and out. There was noise, but it was hard to tell what was happening. Every small truth turned into a wild rumor. Bitty doubted any sparrow would be capable of getting a reliable report, even Walter.

Dawn brightened the landscape. The mood stayed dark as night. A few people slept on the ground, but most stood, their arms linked, their eyes closed.

"Ay!"

At last there was a shout.

Then? A cheer as rescuers led a stumbling miner out of the shaft and into the coal yard.

"Dear God," Jamie's mother said. Two more rescuers came out. They carried, between them, a stretcher, and Jamie's tall father took up every inch of it. His face was black with dust. His body was covered with a blanket.

"Is he dead?" Clarence asked.

"No, look," Bitty said. "His hand!"

Mr. Campbell's right hand dangled from the stretcher, free of the blanket. With his thumb and index finger, he formed a circle; the other fingers stood above it like rays of sunlight.

"Okay," Bitty said. "He's saying he's okay!"

"Yes!" Clarence cried.

Another stretcher came out, but the man upon it didn't move. More stretchers followed.

In the near distance, the church bells rang, celebration and sorrow clanging in harmony. When they stopped ringing, Bo Collins cleared his throat and wiped sweat from his forehead.

"There's five that didn't make it," he said.

Uncle Aubrey counted; that meant they'd saved one, two—seven humans, counting Jamie. Even more if you counted the rescue crew. But five lives lost. No one made a sound as the foreman announced the names of the fallen men. Bitty knew all of them. One name he knew better than the others: Hurley, Steven J. The Gap-Toothed Man.

Chapter 22

The sky was dark the day of the funeral, filled with flat clouds that matched the gray stones in the human cemetery.

"I'll tell you," said Uncle Aubrey as he flew toward a sturdy oak a good distance from the stones, "Florida's starting to sound like a mighty fine idea."

But even on that sad day, and even though he kept claiming that his joints ached as bad as Aunt Lou's, Bitty knew Uncle Aubrey was enjoying his freedom. Couldn't he feel the wind in his wings? Couldn't he see the honeysuckle, in knots and tangles along the railroad tracks? The world could be sad and scary, sure. But it could be thrilling, wondrous and beautiful. The world could be anything they wanted to make it. Bitty was on the verge of pointing this out when he heard his uncle say softly (for it wasn't like him to utter such things out loud): "Even in sorrow: joy."

And so the canaries landed, wrapped in their own private thoughts, on a solid branch of the oak. Bitty thought about Clarence, who'd left for Charleston amid tears and promises and a firm salute from Uncle Aubrey. He thought about the inventor and the politician, who'd just returned to town for the funeral, even though the accident report determined that a roof fall started it all, caused by a weak support beam. He thought about all the funerals he had never been able to attend. And he thought about Mr. Hurley.

The Campbells passed by the tree on their way to the cemetery. Jamie looked up at them and waved. "Ducks on a pond," he said.

"No," said his mother. "They look more like a row of paper dolls."

And what did the humans look like, from where the canaries sat? Eck would have found just the right word for it. Bitty had a jumble of words as he watched the Campbells join the others by the open graves: *sad, angry, respectful, proud.*

The men blew their noses. The women wept openly. Preach, by his father's side, helped lead the readings. *"Ashes to ashes, dust to dust."* The whole sky felt heavy.

"If only..." Bitty started to say, "if only we'd been quicker," but he never finished his sentence. Anyway, it wouldn't have made a difference. Six miners had lived. Five had not. They would have to accept that and move on.

"He was a good man, even if he did squeeze a little hard," Alice said.

The others nodded. Hadn't Mr. Hurley been the first one at work every morning, risking his own life along with theirs? Hadn't he saved Chester when the gas knocked him cold?

"I'm sorry I made fun of the way he ran," Chester said. "Only... only, he really *did* look like an elephant."

"He was a miner," Uncle Aubrey said. "Like us."

The service ended. The mourners milled about, squeezing hands and clapping shoulders. The canaries bowed as the humans passed again under their tree.

But Alice lifted her head.

On the back of his neck, Bitty felt the sort of prickle that told him something was about to happen. Alice opened her mouth and sang—the way canaries used to sing, before the mines and the coal dust and the cages.

Sing, little songbird, safe and sound.
Fly, little songbird, glory bound.

The song wasn't fast, but it wasn't slow, either. It was about the end of life, but it was about new beginnings, too. Bitty found that he knew all the words and joined in. The sweetness of his own voice surprised him. All traces of frogginess and coal dust were gone. Uncle Aubrey joined them with his deep, rich bass, and then every bird in the tree was singing.

Feathers float on yonder wind.
Pain and sorrow now rescind.
Night has fallen, black as coal.
Time has come to rest your soul.
Sing, little songbird, sing.
Sing, little songbird, sing.

Jamie and his family stopped to listen. The Gap-Toothed Man's widow stopped, too. Her eyes were red, but the sharpness went out of her shoulders and she loosened her grip on her handkerchief.

"I don't think I ever did hear a thing so beautiful," she said. "Not ever in this world."

Jamie's ma linked her arm through Mrs. Hurley's. "They are beautiful," she said. "Jamie always promised me they would sing like that."

"Why now, Pa?" Jamie asked. "How come we haven't heard them really sing until now?"

Clayton Campbell put a hand on his son's shoulder. "Could be they just didn't have much of a reason," he said.

Later, much later, when the canaries had gathered back in their tree beyond Jamie's window, Aunt Lou called a meeting.

"I think we should stick around awhile," she said. "For the summer, at least. These people *need* us."

"What about your arthritis?" Bitty asked her. "What about the ocean?"

"The ocean will still be there this winter, when it gets cold," Aunt Lou said. "And Charleston will be there next spring. Right now there's work for us here."

"Work?" repeated Uncle Aubrey. "You'd better believe there's work!" And he set about finding the perfect branch to keep track of the group's singing engagements for the remainder of the season.

Mr. Finch kept his promise. Bitty saw at least two newspaper stories on the need for a conversation about the plight of miners in West Virginia. The union's efforts were always mentioned by the second paragraph; the delegate was mentioned by the third. Nothing had happened yet. A conversation required two sides to do the talking, and so far, no one was talking back. Besides, Uncle Aubrey said, talking wasn't the same as doing. And Bitty knew that while there were plenty of things that could make the miners safer, mining would always be a dangerous job. Still, you had to start somewhere.

The canaries stayed in Coalbank Hollow until the end of September, when they could no longer ignore the whipping wind.

They stayed long enough to see Jamie start school again. (He wanted to win a scholarship, they heard him tell Preach, to study veterinary medicine at Virginia Polytechnic.)

They stayed until the town unveiled a memorial honoring the miners who had died in the No. 7—the miners who had died recently, and the miners who had died long ago. The memorial honored living miners, too, and their years spent working beneath the earth.

The birds watched the ceremony and sang with the school choir under a sky that threatened rain but didn't make good on its threat. When it was all over and the humans had gone, the birds flew to the monument for a closer inspection. The four-foot base bore the names of the men who had died in Coalbank Hollow. Upon the base stood a man wearing a miner's cap. He carried a lunch pail, a pickax and a shovel, and his face wore a look of determination and pride. The detail was so exact that if you looked closely, between his bronze lips, you could see the dim outline of his teeth. And between his front teeth? A gap. Also cast in bronze, near the miner's boots, was a cage. And on top of the cage, with its wings outstretched, was the small figure of a canary. A small plaque beneath the bird bore these words:

For they were so brave that they risked their lives
to save the lives of men.

"I don't know about you guys, but I wasn't brave," Chester said. "I was scared out of my mind."

It was the first time Bitty could remember Chester admitting he was afraid.

"I just figured something out," Bitty said. "Being brave doesn't mean you're not scared. It means you keep on going when you are."

Chester thought about that. "So what you're saying is that if I was *more* scared than the rest of you, that means I was the bravest one. Right?"

"We were *all* brave," Bitty said. His heart swelled with pride even as the September wind ruffled his feathers. Soon they would have to leave this place.

"We'll catch a chill if we stay much longer," said Aunt Lou, echoing his thoughts. She perched above him, on the miner's solid shoulder. "But we'll come back. I'm sure we'll come back."

"A chill?" said Uncle Aubrey, who was perched on the miner's boot. "We have to get moving. We can't risk a chill. Think of what that could do to our voices! Our voices are our livelihoods."

Bitty smiled and shook his head. *Some things never change,* he thought. *But others . . .*

He stood on the tips of his toes and stretched his wings as far as they could go. He didn't hit Chester. Or a perch. Or a metal bar. He didn't hit anything but the crisp September air. He felt like flying.

"Come on," he said to Alice and Chester. "Let's go."

"Where are we going this time?" they asked in unison.

Bitty looked at the clouds, which were parting now, their grieving done. He looked at the blue West Virginia sky.

"Up," he said.

Acknowledgments

Many thanks to Mary Cash for her keen eye and sage voice, and for giving Bitty wings. Thanks to Holiday House, Grace Maccarone, Barbara Perris, and Chris Sheban. It takes a village to publish a book, too; if I didn't know that before, I do now.

When I started writing this story, most people advised against a talking animal middle-grade, so when I gave this manuscript to my agent, it felt like a dare. Thanks, Susan Cohen, for taking it and Brianne Johnson, first believer.

I am grateful to the following people for their coal-mining stories, technical expertise, and general sense of direction: Jerry Asher, Melody Bragg, Joy Lynn, Stuart "Sonny" Schuman, Karen Vuranch, Rachael Walker, and the late Malcolm McPherson. Any mistakes are my own.

I am grateful to the following writers for their friendship, encouragement, and general butt kicking: Tom Angleberger, Cece Bell, Molly Burnham, Margaret Egan, Mary Hill, Leigh Anne Kelley, Anne Marie Pace, and Alicia Potter. Thanks, to critique group members Anamaria Anderson, Moira Rose Donohue, Marfé Ferguson Delano, Marty Rhodes Figley, Anna Hebner, Carla Heymsfeld, Liz Macklin, Suzy McIntire, Martha Taylor, and fearless leader, Jacqueline Jules. I'm especially grateful to Wendy Shang, who read (and reread) this story, often after a frantic, late-night phone call.

Thanks to readers, librarians, archivists, *Roanoke Times*, and my old Bethesda critique group. And a huge thanks to my friends and family for the constant cheerleading and support, especially: Linda and Jimmy Deemer, Harvey and Linda Rosenberg, Andrew Rosenberg and Melanie Ross, and Sally Lazorchak.

To my kids, Graham and Karina: you are my first readers and my first editors. Thank you for the bedtime critique sessions and for always listening; I listened, too. And to my husband, Butch Lazorchak, who gave me the gifts of time and love: Even though you may not think so, they were all I ever needed.

Author's Note

Coalbank Hollow is a fictional town in West Virginia, though I named it after a mine in Blacksburg, Virginia, that was once owned by Murray Slusser, my stepdad's grandfather. The mine closed in the early 1940s, but the name has always captured my imagination. The fictional Coalbank Hollow isn't meant to represent the original mine or its operation in any way. According to Deemer family history, Grandad Slusser was well liked and known for taking care of his miners.

C.Lit PZ 7 .R71897 Can 2013
Rosenberg, Madelyn,
Canary in the coal mine